The Women Without Eyes

Micah Castle

Content warnings are available at the end of this book.
Please consult this list for any particular subject matter you maybe sensitive to.

ISBN: 978-1-960534-25-5 (Paperback)
ISBN: B0DQJ2GV4K (Ebook)

Written by Micah Castle
Edited by Kieran Judge & Kasey Kubica
Cover art by Coversthatkill

Published by Grendel Press LLC
www.grendelpress.com

To my amazing wife, Nikki—without her, none of this would've been possible.

January 11, 1994

William Acerieas

THE STREET LAMP CAST a faint white glow into the car and illuminated the old man's eyes. He wore a brown blazer and gray slacks, and held his old-fashioned pipe in his hand, even though he wasn't going to use it until they returned home.

"Remember when I used to bring you here, Will?"

William smiled and nodded, sitting forward in the passenger seat. "Yes. It was a nice time."

Johnathon glanced through the windshield. The sidewalk weaved around the lake beyond. At night, past the grassy bank, it appeared as though it was a hole in the earth, a hungry abyssal chasm consuming all the light. It was still warm this late into winter. No snow or ice upon the water, no misty breath. A halo of light surrounded his grandfather's bald head. "I remember when we had that picnic. Your parents, you, Donna and I... before, you know."

"It was hot and the ice cream we brought melted before we even got it out, and it ruined one of mom's favorite blankets."

The vivid memory of him sitting with his parents on the floral-patterned blanket, his grandparents looking out over the lake. Warmth spread through William's chest.

Then there was...

He shook his head. "Still don't understand why she insisted on bringing it."

"Women are peculiar. Like the Family Book says. '*Females, our blessed vessels for procreation, are strange in their thoughts and ways.*'"

"If they're as weird as the Book says, why do we choose them? Why not men, if we're more normal?"

"Women see everything, William. *Everything*. They see what we do not and cannot. They view the world in a way that we cannot imagine. Their eyes have the ability, the strength, to reveal what's always there, lurking behind what we believe to be real. For instance, when you believed you got away with drinking one of your father's beers outside. Your mother knew the moment you walked inside what you had done."

"I was grounded for two weeks," William sighed. He'd been taught the Family Book from an early age. Still, he wondered why women were specifically chosen. If they were so much better at knowing things, why were men in power in almost every avenue of life?

But grandfather's an Overseer. He's studied the Book longer than I've been alive. It's not my place to question him. If it's wrong, grandfather wouldn't be doing it. Simple as that.

"What about..."

"Enough with the questions, boy," he said. "Listen."

Footsteps on concrete ended their conversation. Johnathon sat back and peered through the driver's side window. A young woman wearing a Cherry Brooke University sweater and jeans walked down the sidewalk from the city side of the park. She glanced at their parked car and picked up her pace, her ponytail bobbing with her gait.

Johnathon watched intently until she passed the car.

"It's time," he said.

William unbuckled his belt and leaned over into the backseat, grabbing the duffel bag from the floor. He unzipped it and double-checked their supplies.

Ski masks.

Sharpened hunting knife.

Blow torch, tank full.

Lighter.

The Family Crest.

He extended the iron rod to which the crest was attached, the diamond outline, the internal curving lines gleaning under the sodium light, and collapsed it.

Oiled.

Two pairs of plastic gloves.

Dart gun, one dart, full.

Scalpel.

Grapefruit spoon and mason jar.

William handed his grandfather the hunting knife, a pair of gloves, the dart gun, and a ski mask. He took another and put it on. Johnathon watched carefully, ensuring his grandson was thorough, like he taught him, like he was *meant* to be. William checked everything a third time and, satisfied, zipped the bag closed. He turned to Johnathon, who already had his mask on, the knife in his right hand and the door handle in his left. The pipe was in the cup holder.

William nodded.

Johnathon opened the door and pulled himself out of the car. William followed quickly, his hands and face prickly and cold, legs heavy, the duffle slung over his shoulder.

The woman felt the dart in her neck, then no more.

Detective Wolfe

DETECTIVE WOLFE PINNED THE phone between his head and shoulder. He parked his cruiser in the closest empty space he could find and killed the engine.

"I'm sorry. I didn't mean to wake Tabby, but I got—I know I could've, but..." He placed his forehead on the steering wheel and took the phone in his hand. "I know I should've ignored it, but you know how it is, Cindy."

Wolfe closed his eyes and visualized the rage bubbling inside him like boiling water in a pot.

"Look, I have to go. I love you and Tabby." He hung up before his wife had the chance to reply. He chucked it behind him and reclined in his seat. Wolfe rubbed his eyes with his palms, then heaved himself out of the car.

His partner walked up to him through the dewy grass with a cup of coffee, smelling of hazelnut. Detective Toddle wore a pressed white t-shirt, a red tie, and a tan duster and pants. It made Wolfe's wrinkled clothes, thrown on in a hurry, appear even worse.

"You just wake up?" Toddle said.

"Something like that. What's going on?"

"They found a body. A CBU student called it in from a payphone."

"Wonderful."

He walked around Toddle, passed under the police tape, and trudged down to the shoreline. Mist still clung to the calm lake. It was a warm winter day, which was a plus. The victim lay half-in, half-out of the water. Her limbs were placed in a way that reminded Wolfe of someone preparing to make a snow angel. Her dark beige flesh was paled, contrasting with her jet-black hair, spilling from behind her head in a knotty mess of grit and blood. The sweater and jeans she wore looked new, despite the bloody collar and hems soaked past her knees.

A couple of yards away were Martin's team, the medical examiners, placing their gear into thick, black cases. Evidence went into air-tight plastic bags. Police officers stood at the warning tape, keeping the public at bay. There weren't many onlookers, probably due to the early hour, but Wolfe knew there would be more soon.

The examiners worked quickly.

As Wolfe closed in on the victim, nearly slipping on the slope, he stopped. "Shit."

"See it?" Toddle said.

"Her eyes are missing."

Toddle put his hand on Wolfe's shoulder and walked him around the body.

"Why would the killer take her eyes?" Wolfe said.

"A trophy, maybe?"

Wolfe crouched and his knees cracked like twigs. There were no signs of the body being moved: no drag marks or blood in the sand or grass. He didn't check the sidewalk, but he figured that would've been obvious to find by the others. She could've been carried here and dumped after the fact, or led her to the shoreline beforehand, letting the blood wash away in the water...

The eyes seemed like they had been removed by an ice cream scooper, precise and clean. Her throat had similarly been cleanly cut. A pro. Her right sleeve was pulled up to expose a strangely shaped, swollen wound on her wrist.

"Looks professional, doesn't it?" Toddle said, hunkering on the opposite side of the victim.

"No jagged marks. Quick, probably, and smooth. The guy probably used something like a filet knife or scalpel."

"Scalpel," Toddle murmured. "Didn't think of that. I was thinking maybe the kind of knife sushi places use to cut fish."

"That's a filet knife."

"Oh."

"Any witnesses?"

"Not that we know of."

"What about the murder weapon?"

"Not found it."

Wolfe glanced at the lake. "Think he would've tossed it?"

"Maybe." Toddle sipped his coffee. "We can request they drag it, but you know how tight the station's resources are, especially for just one girl."

"Yeah." *Anything to save a few bucks, huh?*

The detective focused back on the victim. He took a pen from his pocket and gently rolled her wrist towards him. "Know anything about this?" From what he could make out, it was a hexagonal shape with twisting lines inside.

"Not much, but she was definitely branded with something, pre- or post-mortem. We won't know until the autopsy."

"Christ," Wolfe hissed.

"My thoughts, too."

Wolfe straightened, trying to veer the conversation away from the hell the poor woman had been put through. "Anyone ID her?"

Toddle pulled out his notepad and flipped to a page of notes. "No one yet. Her purse or wallet, if she carried either, isn't here, either." He looked over his shoulder, then back to his partner.

"I'm guessing she's a college student. No one really takes this path except to get to Cherry Brooke U from downtown. I'd put her in her early twenties."

More onlookers had gathered from the CBU side of the park. A mishmash of plaid pajamas bottoms, slippers, baggy, neon sweatshirts. A handful of them carried disposal cameras.

Leeches will be here soon... Fucking journalists.

"All right," Wolfe said. "Let's get back, make a request, do some digging, and see what Martin says."

January 16, 1994

Detective Wolfe

Toddle and Wolfe's lake drag request was denied, the unofficial excuse being not enough resources to justify a potential murder weapon with only one victim. Budgets had to be cut somewhere. Probably why neither of them had received the ME report yet, either. However, through long phone calls to the administration and faculty at Cherry Brooke University, they believed the victim was Susan Tanaka, a 21-year-old junior majoring in Education. They were given her parents' number and contacted them. They lived outside the city in Mistvale, an hour's drive away, and would be there as soon as possible to ID the body.

When they arrived at the station, Wolfe volunteered to take the Tanakas to the morgue. The mother was short and disheveled, her eyes sunken and bleary. Wolfe could see the resemblance to Susan. Her father's handshake was firm, and he possessed the hard, blank stare of a man who had seen things he never wished to see again.

Quietly, they stood before the viewing window. A tall, brunette ME stood behind a metal table covered by a white sheet. She looked at Wolfe.

"Are you ready?" Wolfe asked the parents.

Her father nodded, arms around his wife, who gave no recognition to his question.

The ME pulled back the sheet to reveal Susan's face, her hair clean of mud and blood, her lips pale blue. Her eyes were closed as if she were only sleeping. The mother's knees gave way. She clawed at her husband's shirt, trying her best to stay standing through her sobbing. Susan's father peered vacantly through the glass.

"Is this her?" the examiner said through the intercom.

A moment passed. Two.

The father nodded.

The ME covered the victim, then closed the window curtain. In the reflection, Wolfe saw Susan's father blinking back tears. Before leaving the morgue, they stopped at the closed double doors.

"I'm sorry to have to do this," Wolfe said, "but I have to ask you some questions."

The father nodded. Susan's mother had quieted but kept her face buried in her husband's chest.

"Did Susan have any boyfriends?"

"No," he said.

"Any close friends we could talk to?"

"No. Susan wasn't social. She only cared about her work."

"Enemies? Not just hers, but of your family's."

He shook his head. "We keep to ourselves."

Wolfe's mouth dried. "I hate asking, but where were you two last night?"

The father's brow furrowed. "You think *we* could have done this?"

"No," he quickly said. "But we *have* to ask. Just procedure."

"We were at home," the man spat. "Sleeping."

The detective almost asked: "Can anyone vouch for that?" but kept it to himself. It was clear they weren't responsible, and driving an hour to and from the park to kill their daughter was absurd. No motive. No reason.

"All right, that's all I need. Thank you." Wolfe popped open the door for them.

Outside, the overcast was gray, but no flakes yet. Wolfe pulled his collar up and braced himself against the wind. Before getting into his cruiser, he watched the parents walk to their car, the husband almost carrying his trembling wife.

He wanted to run up to them and apologize, knew that he *should*, and tell them he would do all in his power to catch the guy who did this. But he always felt like a patronizing jackass when he said sorry to anyone who lost someone, especially to parents who weren't parents anymore. A stranger saying, "Sorry for your loss," wouldn't make anything better. They would still drive home in a silence broken only by crying. The father would wander upstairs into his little girl's empty room, their memories together playing through his mind, sit on her bed, and break down. Susan's father appeared composed now, but the moment he was alone, Wolfe knew the pain would take over.

Wolfe got in his car.

"How'd it go?"

Wolfe sunk into his chair. He ran his hand through his thinning hair. "As you'd expect."

Toddle nodded. "Sorry."

"Part of the job."

"Don't know if it helps, but we finally got the ME report. A copy's on your desk."

"Should've just given it to me while I was there," he murmured. He picked up the manila folder with Susan's name written on it. The top page had a photo of her face stapled to it. He ignored it as he read.

Her toxicology was almost clean. Not a drop of alcohol, but there were high levels of procaine and benzodiazepine. In the footnotes: *Not certain which specific drug was in her system, but likely a very strong sedative. It's possible she took it prior to the attack, but unlikely. An injection point was found on the right side of her neck. Need more information to be 100%.*

She wasn't raped, nor had she been pregnant. No semen found, nor any DNA, fingerprints, or skin fragments left by the killer. Nothing under the fingernails, so there wasn't a struggle.

Estimated time of death was around 3 AM, four hours before she was found.

Some nerve tissue remained in the eye sockets, but it appeared that the killer dislodged the eye before cutting the optic nerves and muscles. Besides that, there was no damage, internal or external, to the skull.

The slash through her neck killed her, causing blood loss and eventual asphyxiation. The blade cut through the left external jugular vein, sternomastoid muscle, left common carotid artery, and through the opposite side.

Wolfe didn't understand the scientific jargon, but he imagined what the slash looked like: left to right.

"Killer's right-handed," he muttered.

The brand on her right wrist was done postmortem. It wasn't like cattle branding irons. Those were wide and thick, and the symbol here wasn't simple, like something farmers might use. A monochrome photo of the wrist, cleaned of burnt flesh, was clipped to the paper. A diamond with lines weaving up from the point at the bottom, connecting with the outer lines, then veering and falling back down, their ends combining with the diagonal sides.

Wolfe looked up when Captain Conti opened his office door. His white t-shirt was a size too small, his undershirt clearly seen through it, and his suspenders were too tight. He wiped his bald head with a handkerchief.

"Toddle, Wolfe."

"Yeah, Captain?" Toddle said.

"They found a body out on the upper south side, in an abandoned house on Dutch Ave."

"What's that got to do with us?" Wolfe said.

"Apparently, this guy is a relative of someone important. God knows who or for what, but the Commander just told me to get some of my people out there, pronto."

"So, they want us to cover something up? Drugs? Hookers? *Gay love affair*?" Toddle grinned.

"I'm not asking you to cover anything up. If the guy's found fucking other guys with coke falling out his nose, just make a report and I'll deal with it."

Wolfe closed Susan's labs, slapped a sticky note onto the cover, opened the bottom drawer of his cabinet and slid it in. He didn't want it to be lost among the other folders. "So just go and check it out?"

Conti nodded. "Keep everything on the up and up. Remember, shit rolls downhill, and if someone screws up, no matter how high they are, we all get shit on."

FEBRUARY 10, 1994

William Acerieas

ETCHED INTO THE TOP of the onyx tombstone was his name: *Johnathon Acerieas Jr.* Below was the Family Crest, and under that, dates: *October 11, 1948 — January 28, 1994.* By his grandfather's grave was his grandmother's—*Donna Acerieas*—and next to hers were his parents: *Gregory Acerieas* and *Alicia Acerieas.* His mother's and father's bodies were beneath him, but what made them who they were in life, were not. It didn't give William any solace.

He wiped his eyes, looked over his shoulder and found no one around. Loneliness and relief washed over him. The funeral had only been open to family, and William was the only one who came. Grandfather's siblings passed on ages ago, and what few relatives he had, if they were still alive, were in parts unknown.

The fresh earth was lightly dusted. He moved around the hillock and put his palm to the sleek, cold surface of the tombstone. "Goodbye, Grandfather."

He crossed the frosted grass and got into the car he inherited. Snow melted on the window as he left the cemetery, turning left at the wrought iron gate towards their—*his*—home.

That's not all grandfather left me.

He rested a hand on the envelope in his pocket.

Inside the empty Victorian house, the silence was palpable. William unhooked his cuffs, removed his red tie and black overcoat and draped them over the back of a kitchen chair. He drifted from one room to another, flittering memories passing by. *This is where father taught me to play cards, and this is where mother showed me how to tie a tie before a dinner at the University. Grandfather snuck me a sip of wine during dinner when grandmother wasn't looking, and she used to let me bake cookies with her, and she'd make me cocoa after coming in from the snow...*

The mahogany grandfather clock in the living room echoed through the home. He decided he shouldn't waste any more time. The Family's Work now rested on his shoulders. At the sliding doors in the living room, he stared at the keyholes. Wind howled outside. Rain spat on the windows.

William had waited for this day ever since he was taught the Work, the responsibility he held in his hands. His stomach churned and he tasted bile at the back of his throat. Swallowing the sour taste, he removed the envelope from his pocket, undid the flap, and pulled out the rusted copper key. He put it in the lock with trembling fingers and, despite the nerves, turned his wrist.

He slide open both doors and stopped in the doorway of his grandfather's study. *His* study.

"Only men of age can pass," his grandfather would say with a smirk when he asked before his sixteenth birthday. It was a made-up rule, he knew, because he had been in there many times before then, but after he came of age, he was inside the study's book-lined walls constantly. It still felt like new terrain to him now, an unknown land.

William walked into the center of the room. It still smelt of him, smoke and tobacco. It was never pleasant, but comforting. Each row brimmed with thick tomes, passed down relics of times long before William's parents were a thought between his grandparents.

In Abissum Incomprehensiblem et Ultra, the Family Book, lay open on the dark wood podium by the far wall. Half-melted candles remained on black steel pedestals in the four corners of the room. The gray door in the eastern wall closed. It was as though grandfather had just left for a moment and would soon return. William glanced at the open doors in the hopes the cancer had been nothing but a dream, but his gaze was met by cold, empty reality.

Turning his attention back to the Book, he imagined his grandfather leaning over the pedestal, his calloused fingers holding the wood as he spoke the forgotten language. He spoke of passing, of the Beyond, of the unimaginable transformative power hidden in the Other Place, a world in which his Family had attempted to form a bridge to for many years but always failed to build.

The Family ran dry, a generation practically exhausted, and were forced to wait until the new generation was born, raised, taught by the Overseers, and became harbingers of the Family's cause like those before them. Many were selfish, however, all going to the Other Place without leaving behind a child, or abandoning the Family entirely to live as recluses in the far reaches of the world. There had been talk of using others to make the connection, but only the Acerieas line was pure, was *worthy*, so the Book said. William was the only one left of the new generation, the only one to complete his grandfather's work.

Nausea lapped at his mouth. He scratched his forehead, bit his bottom lip.

"How am I supposed to do it alone?" he asked the empty room, already knowing the answer.

He lifted the Family Book's back cover, revealing another key inlaid into the podium.

He took it and unlocked the gray door. Pale light from the living room reached the stairwell, but the gloom was too dense to fully penetrate. William didn't need light. He knew the stairs, knew the turn halfway down, knew there were only a few steps before he was on solid ground. His breath turned to mist. Then there was the doorway remaining from the old brick foundation, and past that, his grandfather's workshop.

He flicked on the floodlight.

The renovated cellar was higher than anyone, except his grandfather, anticipated. William remembered his father saying it was as if he had built a foundry with dirt, but his grandfather was adamant it was necessary for the family cause, that the Machine he created would bring a new technological age.

Large glass vats were filled with a peridot liquid, illuminated by lights inside. The fluid was a mixture of chemicals and liquefied materials his grandfather concocted. Nobody knew exactly what the mixture was; he took what he called the 'recipe' to the grave. The substance fueled the Machine and preserved the Offerings until use.

The Offerings his grandfather had obtained since his mother's passing rested at the bottom of the containers. They floated when William would increase the current from the generator in the back. They would boil and disintegrate, break down, and then the mixture would run through tubing from the discs to a copper helmet attached to an old wooden chair.

William crossed over the Family Crest carved into the floor, where, if successful, the connection would appear. Branching the two worlds and severing the shackles of reality, it would allow passage from one to another. The Book said an unblemished world dwelled on the other side where most of his family were, including his parents. A better place with tools and knowledge to transcend the Family into beings which could break the tethers of humanity and bend not only that world, but *this one*, to their will. Time and space would only be words to them. His grandfather had likened it to a tangible Heaven.

William touched the coarse wood of the armrest, then strolled to the nearby vat and placed his palm to the glass. Tears fell down his shallow cheeks.

This is no longer his.

It's mine.

FEBRUARY 24, 1994

Detective Wolfe

WOLFE FELT LIKE HE hadn't had a full night's sleep in over a year, but it had only been a little over a month since the first reports of George Meyer's murder broke. He was the son of Henry Meyer, CEO of Sicher Banking, who donated seven-figures to several political campaigns. George Meyer was only the beginning of the string of murders.

Wolfe's precinct covered the upper south side and lower north side, but every precinct was dumbfounded by how to the South Side Killer (SSK), given the name due to the initial murders starting on the south side. There were all were put onto their killings, running hotlines and crossing jurisdictions willy-nilly. Every time they thought they had an idea of where the killer would strike next, a body would appear somewhere else. The ones they could *find*. Soon it wouldn't matter who was from where because the FBI would be coming down from DC if they couldn't end it quick.

He (they presumed the killer was a man) wasn't prejudiced or discriminatory or after big names. No matter how much money they have, or what sex, age, or race they were, he put them in the grave. What turned a one-off murder to a serial was how they were done. The victims were bound by their ankles and wrists with dress ties, mostly satin, or faux leather belts. If it were a man his genitalia were also bound, if it were a woman, their breasts. Both the belt and ties were easily bought from most clothing stores. Once tied-up, he put them into a bathtub or shower, cleaned them from head-to-toe with a toothbrush inside and out, then cut their throat with what they believed to be a box cutter or similar tool.

That's where they always found them, soaking wet in a pink-stained tub, cleaned thoroughly pre-mortem. Toothbrush bristles were found inside every victim, with no other penetration. Like everything about the SSK, the brushes were common and could be bought anywhere.

Wolfe rolled out of bed, groaned, and sat on the edge of the mattress. Cindy's spot was empty. She had already gotten up and left with Tabby for her grandparents' house, leaving her there while Cindy visited an old friend from college.

He yawned and stood; lower back dully throbbing.

His cell rang.

Cindy.

He let it go to voicemail and trudged into the bathroom to grab a shower.

The precinct was in a frenzy. Seemingly every officer and detective carried folders and evidence bags from one desk to another, from one side of the building to the other, going downstairs or coming up. The janitor worked overtime to keep the floor dry, though everyone's shoes still squeaked. Voices blurred together like white noise. Wolfe pushed through the throng to his desk covered in papers, a stack of files sitting on top.

His chair whined when he sat, setting his coffee on a collection of lab reports. He looked for a pen but couldn't find one. Wolfe reached down to a cabinet and pulled it open, ruffling through it without bothering to look. He stopped when he felt a sticky note on a folder. He put it in front of him and opened it.

"Susan Tanaka."

He remembered her. Not as a person, but what was done to her. The missing eyes, the cut throat, the brand on her wrist. He hadn't thought about her since the SSK began, and wondered if anyone had made any headway on finding *her* killer.

"Toddle!" he shouted across the station.

His partner appeared at his side, his wrinkled shirt sticking out of his khakis.

"Yeah?"

"Susan Tanaka. Remember her?"

Toddle pinched the bridge of his nose. "Uh... Susan Tanaka... Susan Tanaka..."

"Missing eyes."

"Oh, yeah, I remember her. Found her at Refleski Park, right?"

Wolfe nodded. "Did anyone make any headway on the case?"

His partner shook his head. "With everything going on, I don't think anyone had the time to look into anything else. Can't blame them."

Wolfe sighed. Before dropping the file back into the cabinet, he wrote on the note: '**DON'T FORGET!**'

There goes another one pushed aside.

Wolfe didn't have chance to check Cindy's voicemail until well into the evening. He dropped into his car, pulled the door closed, took out his phone and played the message.

"Hey honey, it's me. Just got done dropping Tabby off. Mom and Dad say hi, and hope we can join them at their beach house this summer. Anyway, I'm meeting Greg at the Smoldering Café, then I think we're going to be walking around downtown. Don't worry, I won't spend too much." Cindy laughed. *"I'll be home around six, and you know what I was thinking? Tabby can stay the night at my parents' and we can have the night alone. Celebrate Valentine's Day like we were supposed to. Just you... me... our special rum."* She laughed. *"Call me when you can. Love you."*

The voicemail ended.

He smiled as he shut the phone. He hadn't looked at the time all day. At mid-afternoon another SSK killing had been reported on the upper east side, and he'd been called in to assist. Heading back to the station he'd had another call about a possible sighting on the west side and they needed him there, too. Then, there was paperwork.

But he was sure it wasn't too late. He could make it home in time before Cindy fell asleep. His numb hand jittered as he started the car, cranking the heat. The dashboard came to life with multicolored lights.

10:08 PM.

"Shit."

It was 10:45 PM by the time he made it home. All the lights were off, and not bothering with their special rum hidden in a kitchen cabinet, he slipped upstairs. The bedroom door was ajar.

Cindy was asleep on her back, wearing a black, lacy teddy he had bought for her a few anniversaries ago. Her brunette hair was tied back, and he could tell when he got close that she had shaved her legs that day. The lavender perfume she wore radiated off her body.

He made for the bathroom and sat on the toilet with his face in his hands.

Why does it always have to be like this?

Work before Cindy.

Before Tabby.

Before everything.

Why don't I quit?

I should find some low-demanding job at a store or wherever. The budget would be tight but we could manage, get food stamps if we have to. We could survive.

I don't have *to be a detective. I don't* have *to be a cop at all.*

But he knew he wouldn't quit. He couldn't sit by and let murders happen and nothing come of it. Without him, more would fall through the cracks, more would go uninvestigated. Without him, countless lives would fall into the abyss without so much as a second glance.

And the killers. They need put away or put down. Nothing else about it.

Wolfe sat back against the tank. He wiped his eyes on his sleeve, sighed, and got ready for bed.

He entered the bedroom in a t-shirt and boxer briefs, and quietly got under the covers.

"I love you," he whispered, and kissed Cindy's forehead. He rolled over and allowed sleep to take him.

MARCH 11, 1994

William Acerieas

HE TAPPED HIS FINGERS against his shaking leg and stared through the windshield at the squat, gray building. Unlike most places, security cameras hadn't been installed here, yet. Relieved, he sat back in the driver's seat to avoid the streetlight, hiding in the shadows.

The Cherry Brooke Public Library had been closed since 9 PM. She was still inside doing God knows what.

Always busy, Mrs. Davis.

His grandfather had instructed him time and again to choose random people for the Offerings, those without any ties to the Family. That was difficult, often nearly impossible. William couldn't simply pick a stranger from the masses. He felt those with emotional bonds would be stronger and therefore increase the chances for those in the Other World to return. That was what he told himself. Familiarity was important, even if he didn't recognize it.

Grandfather wasn't always right, anyway.

Thus, he had chosen his childhood librarian, Mrs. Davis. It had been a decade since he last saw her, and from what he knew she retired years ago, but still volunteered. He assumed she felt the library was a child she refused to abandon, even once the doors of her career closed.

William smiled and closed his eyes.

He held his mother's hand as they walked through the double-doors into the carpeted entryway and then on through another set of doors towards the polished counter of the librarian.

Mrs. Davis spoke briefly to his mother before leaning over the desk, looking down at him with gray-blue eyes behind gold rimmed glasses. She smiled.

"Are you ready for today, Willy? Your friends are already here."

He nodded.

His mother crouched to his height, adjusted the collar of his shirt. Her auburn hair spilled over her pale shoulders and curled around her pronounced collarbone. "You going to be good today, William?"

He nodded, again.

She ran her fingers through his hair. "Good boy. Now, don't act up for Mrs. Davis, and make sure to share with the other children."

He nodded a third time.

"I'll be back in a few hours."

"Will daddy be here, too?" he said.

She blinked, smiling. "No, no honey, he won't. I'm sorry, but he's... he's busy, you know? He'll be here soon."

"Promise?"

"Promise." She wrapped her arms around him and squeezed him against her thin body. She released him, and Mrs. Davis took his hand and escorted him towards the children's section of the library. He looked back to his mother standing there, eyes red-rimmed, cheeks wet.

A door slammed shut, and he opened his eyes and sat up. Mrs. Davis turned away from the library, her large purse hung over her shoulder. She wore a maroon overcoat and a blue dress hanging to her ankles. William was surprised how strong she looked at her age as she walked across the salted parking lot without a stick or a limp. She had to be at least 70-years-old.

Hustling, he removed the gloves from the duffle and pulled them on. He took the hunting knife and slid it up his left jacket sleeve, then got out of the car, nearly falling face-first onto the tarmac. His legs prickled, waking up. He checked over his shoulder. The street was empty.

"Mrs. Davis!"

The woman stopped, looked, and met his smile with her own. "Willy? Willy Acerieas? Is that *you*?"

Up close, he stood a foot taller than her. "It's me. How've you been?"

"What are you doing here, at this hour?"

"Well, my grandfather passed, you know, and it had me wondering how you were doing."

She rubbed his arm. "I heard. Such a shame. Cancer, wasn't it? He donated a lot to the library, helped a lot of kids. I'm so sorry, but you should've come sooner. The library's closed and I'm heading home now, maybe tomorrow afternoon we can have tea or coffee, if you like?"

He inhaled sharply. "That sounds good, thank you."

"No need, Willy." She waved her hand. "Now, will you be a gentleman and help an old lady to her car? It's over there." She pointed to an old Corolla in the corner of the lot, the spaces either side clear of snow.

He put out his arm, which she took, and they walked to the car.

"So, how have you been?"

"As good as I can be, I suppose. You?"

"Oh, doing fine, doing fine. Can't complain too much."

They arrived at her vehicle. He pulled his arm away as she dug into her purse. He glanced around. The street was still deserted.

"Damn keys," she said. "Always getting lost in this thing."

William bent his left hand back, opened his palm. The knife slid into his grip.

"Found them!" She turned to him with the keys raised like discovered treasure. Her eyes widened, open mouth froze. "What are you...?"

William slashed with the knife, ripping through her neck. He got closer to her, ensuring the blade cut all the way through to the open air on the opposite side. His hands trembled. His stomach knotted. When his grandfather did it, it was different, as if William wasn't truly there. Doing it himself felt terrifying, enthralling. Fear and excitement clashed, adrenaline surging through his veins. He wanted to smile and cry, vomit and cheer. He stepped away from her deflating body and watched, transfixed.

Mrs. Davis's eyes remained wide, her jaw slack, as though stuck permanently surprised by the boy she once watched over taking away her life. Rivulets of blood spilled from her neck, cascading down her clothes. She stumbled back, slipped on her own blood, and crashed against her car, sliding down the metal with a wet, metallic whine until she fell to the ground. Gasping, chest hitching, she held her neck as if she could plug the hole, before her body rattled and finally stilled.

He inspected his blood-splattered clothes. It was surprising so much came out from such a little, old woman. He was glad he packed a change of clothes.

Car.

William checked the street was deserted, then sprinted back to his car, got in, and jabbed the key into the ignition with a trembling hand.

Should have parked next to her. How could I overlook this?

He backed into the spot next to Mrs. Davis.

It doesn't matter now. I'll do better next time.

Breath heavy, face numb, he leapt out with the duffel. Scanned the supplies quickly: blowtorch and starter, grapefruit spoon, mason jar, scalpel, Family Crest. He looked over the retired librarian.

A twinge of guilt strung in his chest, but he ignored it and began harvesting.

He couldn't stop smiling, and his heart drummed on his sternum. His body tingled.

Grandfather would be so proud of me. The whole family would be. My first Offering!

He checked the side mirror. No one was behind him. He threw on the turn signal. Swinging the car around the corner, Mrs. Davis's eyes shook in the mason jar in the cup holder.

It had been messier than he imagined. He'd seen his grandfather do it several times, and he made it look easy, but it was far more difficult doing it on his own. Eyes were hard to pop out from their sockets and keep intact, like a pimple refusing to give no matter the pressure. He probably damaged the nerves or the eye itself, but at a glance they seemed normal, and the sockets weren't important.

Removing them had also posed an unexpected problem. His grandfather had been quick with the scalpel. One, two, or sometimes three slices if he was tired, and they were free. For whatever reason, William had to saw through Mrs. Davis's nerves like they were too overdone steak. His forearm still throbbed.

He stopped at a red light and turned on the radio. Bach's *Symphony in G minor No. 6* played. He let the music to wash over him.

Once they were severed, everything had become a blur, surroundings forgotten. Carrying her to the lamppost.

Positioning her like the Family Book illustrated as the brand heated up under the blowtorch. Using that time to change into clean clothes.

The brand was white hot by the time he was dressed. He took the tool and pressed it into her wrist, giving a high-pitched squeal. His hand jerked away when he heard footsteps and someone talking, salt and ice crunching. No time to correct the crest, he tossed everything into the bag, hurried back to his car, and floored it out of the parking lot.

He didn't know if he had been seen. Maybe they'd seen his license plate? He checked the mirrors a dozen times, but the street remained empty. He briefly considered the adrenaline and excitement had caused an auditory hallucination, but if there *had* been someone, they wouldn't have been close to the car. William would've noticed *that*.

What's done is done.

William smelled the burned lining of his soaked duffel. He looked around and was relieved to find an unopened bottle of water in the passenger side cup holder. Tipped it over the brand to stop the whole bag melting.

The light turned green. He took a handful of unnecessary turns, hoping that if he was being followed, he'd lose them. Eventually, he turned into the alley and backed into the gravel driveway. He turned off the engine and the silence of the night weighed over him. The thrill dissolved with each breath and soon the cold enveloped him. Alone, the last to complete such an act, tears blurred his vision.

I wish you here... I wish everyone was here...

Composing himself, he used the back of his hand to wipe his nose and eyes, and coughed into his arm. Now wasn't the time to stew in loss, to let himself drift into the depression pressing just beneath the surface. There was work to do.

"By the Book, the connection will be made. I will be with them again."

In the side room in the basement, he sat on a stool and placed his elbows on the old workbench. The bloodied clothes ran in the washer upstairs, and Mrs. Davis's purse was tucked into a box beneath the worktable next to a bag of dry cement. The duffel bag sagged against a crooked bookcase holding empty mason jars, containers of gasoline, boxes of latex gloves, CO_2 cartridges, and other odds-and-ends.

Yawning, straightening, he sleepily looked over the dirty tools before him.

Blowtorch needs refilled. Brand needs cleaned. Knife also needs to be cleaned, and sharpened, so does the scalpel. Would it be easier to buy a new one, instead?

The tranquilizer gun hung near a rusted hatchet and two sets of chains, one thicker than the other. His grandfather only had five darts for the gun. He said they were filled with a drug he obtained in the '60s and claimed it could knock out a rhino. William wasn't sure if he was lying.

Should I use it for the next one? It'd make it easier. Mrs. Davis wasn't much trouble, but the next could be.

"No," he spat. His grandfather used it because he had gotten older, his body no longer as strong as it once was. William wouldn't use something that could muddle his Offerings.

I'm twenty-three. I don't need something like that.

Sighing, he turned to the bag, still reeking of blood, flesh, and burnt plastic.

"I'll probably have to buy a new one of you, too."

MARCH 12, 1994

Detective Wolfe

Wolfe looked up from his papers when Toddle, holding his phone to his chest, shouted to him. He rubbed his red-rimmed eyes. "What?"

"Got a body at the library."

"SSK?"

"Doesn't sound like it. It was found outside."

"Okay, so?"

"You wanna take it or should I tell 'em to look elsewhere?"

"No, we'll take it." *Don't want another pushed off to someone who'll probably do the bare minimum.*

Toddle spoke for a moment, then hung up and grabbed his hat and coat. Wolfe gulped down the rest of his lukewarm coffee.

"They say anything else?"

"It wasn't covered up or hidden. Just sitting out there, plain as day. Weird, huh?"

"Kinda, yeah."

"The South Side Killer is still at large. His most recent killing was Corianne Jeffries, 28. She was a wife, a mother of one, and taught pre-school at West Side Headstart. This is the SSK's third victim and the police are no closer to apprehending him than they were..."

Wolfe killed the radio as they approached the Cherry Brooke Public Library blocked off by police tape. He parked across the street and got out, Toddle following. Wolfe ducked under the tape and stopped, déjà vu washing over him.

The body of the black female sat cross-legged against a lamppost near an alley which ran between the library and an abandoned store. Her arms were stretched behind her back, wrapped around the lamppost, hands firmly holding her forearms. It reminded Wolfe of a yoga pose. Coagulated blood stained the snow and ice.

And her eyes.

"They're gone," he said.

Detective Wilkinson, wearing a yellow windbreaker tucked into auburn pants, hurried over with a notepad and pen. "I spoke to the man who found her, and he thinks he saw the perp. Nice guy, sort of shook up though. I also spoke to Mrs. Bury, the head librarian."

"What'd she say?" Wolfe said.

Wilkinson scratched his brow with his thumb and looked at his notes. "She knew the victim, apparently for a while. Timara Davis. She used to be the head librarian before retiring. Now does, did, volunteer."

"And the witness?" Toddle said.

He flipped a page. "His name is Brenton Kirkpatrick. He said he was walking last night and saw a car speeding out from the library parking lot. He didn't get a good look but said he was pale, looked tall, with dark hair. Didn't catch the plates. I'm bringing him down to the precinct for a run with the sketch artist as soon as I'm done here."

Wilkinson closed the notepad and slid it into his pocket.

"Thanks," Wolfe said.

He moved to the victim. If he had to guess, he'd put Tamira between 65-years-old and 70-years-old. Her eyes had been scooped out, and a clean line ran across her wrinkled throat. Blood soaked her blue dress, turning it a deep purple.

"Jesus," Toddle hissed. "This is *definitely* not SSK."

"No shit." Wolfe knelt.

Her fingers and fingernails were clean, so there hadn't been an apparent fight. No bruising, either. *The ME might find something I can't see.* Wolfe leaned to the side, peering into the alley, an empty parking lot covered in snow at the end. Around him were shuttered storefronts. People in beanies and scarves gawked at the crime scene on the adjacent sidewalk. A news van pulled up and people piled out like they were preparing to storm a beach. Moments later, a second van showed up.

Leeches.

"How'd this happen in public?" he said.

"Bastard got lucky," Toddle said. "Look at how much blood there is on the snow, and that car over in the parking lot, and here on the lamp post."

"So, he kills her in the library parking lot, then moves her and positions her on the lamppost?"

"Or she was just passing by and got snatched from the alley." Toddle walked to the mouth of the alleyway. "Maybe he was parked over there and simply waited here. Then when she passed, he got her, took her to his car, did it, then set her up here."

"That doesn't make sense. Look." He pointed at the cracked cement of the alley. "There's no blood there; and no footprints. Plus, I doubt he carried her all the way to the lamp post, and *only* cleaned up over there. And if what Wilkinson said was right, the guy's skinny. She's not big, but you'd have to be pretty strong to carry anyone besides a kid all the way here fast enough to not be caught."

Toddle looked at the roof of the library. "How does a place like this not have cameras?"

"Probably can't afford them. Doesn't matter now." They stood quiet for a moment. "Why here? Why her?"

Toddle shook his head. "I dunno..."

A memory crossed his mind. "Remember that case from January, Tanaka something?"

Susan Tanaka's age, location of the body, and what was done to her came back to him. The 'DON'T FORGET!' note flashed through his mind. Still, it felt like he was missing something important. He tried to remember but it eluded him.

"At the lake," Toddle said.

"She was missing her eyes, too," Wolfe said.

"Think it's the same guy?"

"Not many people going around taking eyes, is there?"

"Not that I know of."

They fell into silence and, without speaking, decided there wasn't much left to do there. They needed the police reports, forensic reports, and the witness statement, but they'd have to wait for those. Wolfe and Toddle walked back to the cruiser, ignoring the guppies desperate for a nibble of information. Before they got in, Toddle's cell phone chirped.

"Hold on," he said, removing it from his pocket. "Yeah, yeah. Really? We have something here already. Uh huh, okay. I'll be there soon." He clamped the phone shut. "Another one they want us to look at. Upper south side at the Wheatley." He nodded to the library. "You get back to the precinct and take this one. I'll head over to this new one and then grab a ride back from someone there."

"SSK?"

"With how this day is already going I wouldn't doubt it."

William Acerieas

WILLIAM RECLINED, STARING OUT at the frozen Refleski Lake past the sidewalk and snow laden grass of the park. Families strolled down the shoveled walkway, a father with his son, gloved-hand in gloved-hand, a mother and daughter wearing matching winter outfits, parents flanking a boy focused on his Game Boy. Couples sat on benches as kids had snowball fights.

He recalled the day at the park his grandfather spoke about that night, one of the last times they were together. William breathed deep in the crisp morning air, his thoughts turning to the young woman whose name he later learned from the obituaries: Susan Tanaka.

A freshman at Cherry Brooke University.

Daughter of Brent and Nina Tanaka.

No siblings, only her and her parents in Mistvale.

She was a part of...

He hushed his thoughts.

An Offering's an Offering. Who they were before isn't a concern.

William recalled the way his grandfather pounced that night once the drug took hold, like a lion. He remembered him carrying her to the lake, the knife slicing through her throat, the blood spilling, washing into the water, gleaming under the streetlamp. The eye removal and the smell of burning skin whistling beneath the brand, then positioning her before they took their leave.

Finishing the memory, he looked over his shoulder, reversed out from his space, and entered the fray of traffic.

The nape of William's neck prickled as he passed the library. Goosebumps ran up his arms. It was like he was a fundamental part of its history, memories of his childhood, his mother, and his Offering intertwining. As he stopped at the sign at the corner, he realized there was nowhere to park along the right side. Onlookers and news station crews crowded the sidewalks. Police barriers and yellow tape shielded the left side. The library's lot were clustered with officers, people in dark blue windbreakers, and others he couldn't place.

A police cruiser shielded where Amanda had been placed from view. He couldn't tell if her body was still there or if they moved it already. Nearby, a pudgy man in a neon yellow coat spoke to a tall man with a cell phone.

Is that who saw me last night?

His lungs froze. He faced ahead, refusing to look back.

Despite being proud of his first harvest, the next one he had to be more selective. Until now, William hadn't considered his Family's Work abruptly ending by law enforcement. He knew they investigated the scenes left purposefully behind, but his grandfather had always assured him they'd never be arrested.

"We're always three steps ahead," he would say.

But he wasn't around anymore, and William's sloppiness with Mrs. Davis couldn't happen again. If he was caught, the goal his family had pursued would all be for naught. Wasted. Spoiled. And it would be his fault; he'd be the failure.

The next one must be my last.

Vaguely, he remembered that in the Book it spoke about the quality of Offerings, something about the quality of life converted to energy. William was too flustered to recall much of it.

"Hey asshole, move!" A man behind honked his horn. Hitting the turn signal, William fought the urge to slam the pedal to the floor.

Detective Wolfe

IT FELT LIKE WOLFE drove on autopilot, his mind in a distant place. The streets became a blur of garbage cans overflowing into slush, debris-cluttered alcoves of abandoned businesses, heavily-bundled people sitting on graffitied benches holding cardboard signs. Toddle talked but he heard none of it. His thoughts on the two women. Tamira and Susan. Their missing eyes, their slashed throats, their positioned bodies.

Are they being targeted?

Is this racial? Neither are white.

Did both know the killer? If so, where, how? Significant others? Friends? Colleagues? Co-workers?

Why the park?

Why the library?

Why their eyes?

Why there?

Why them?

There wasn't enough information yet, and he knew barely anything about the killer besides what the witness had told Wilkinson.

His throat tightened; palms clammy.

Was Davis going to be like Tanaka, lost among a sea of papers in his desk as more work came in? Hell, he nearly forgot about Tanaka and that was only a couple months ago. So many reports every day and many never got the attention they deserved, be it domestic abuse, homicides, suicides; anything that required footwork and paperwork. Some weren't even investigated beyond a quick glance and the routine questions to friends and family.

Added to that, with the SSK on the loose, Wolfe didn't want to imagine how many more victims there were that he didn't, couldn't, know about. In the pit of his stomach, he knew there wasn't enough time in the day and energy in his bones to bring them all to justice. He was only one man.

"Wolfe? Wolfe! Stop!"

Jolted back to reality, Wolfe slammed on the brakes, tires screeching. They jerked forward, seatbelts digging into their chests. A young woman in an oversized blue sweater stood in front of a parked car, wide-eyed. Toddle waved her along with his left hand.

"Shit." Toddle rubbed his chest. "What was that?"

Wolfe shook his head. "Was thinking about something. Sorry. Why'd you scream?"

"Because you almost hit that girl," he said, "and I've been telling you to slow down for about a block now. Man, that really hurt."

The driver behind him laid on his horn.

"I'll just get out here."

Wolfe watched him run around the hood of the car, squeeze through the police cruisers already parked along the sidewalk, and make his way into the seedy complex across the street.

The Captain stood in his office doorway. His phone was ringing inside. The faint smell of smoke and whiskey drifted out behind him. "Got anything?"

"Toddle's still there." Wolfe said. "We split our time, worked out better that way."

"I was hoping you'd have something." He knocked on the doorframe. "What about the girl at the library?"

"Not the SSK, but there was a similar one we had back in January." Wolfe hung his jacket on the back of the chair, then dropped into it. "The vic at the library could be a start to another serial."

The Captain stood by Wolfe's desk. "You sure?"

"Not a hundred percent, maybe ninety-five it's the same guy. I haven't got the reports on the second one, but I'd say same person."

"I hope as to shit it's not. Practically everyone in the damn city is being used to catch SSK on top of the regular BS. We're not New York, we don't have endless bodies to throw at this." The Captain rubbed his bald head, then pointed at Wolfe. "Just, uh, when you get the reports, let me know." He went back into his office.

Toddle hurried into the station.

"Was it who we thought it was?" Wolfe said.

He shook his head. "Not in the slightest. Handed it to sex crimes."

"Cap was looking for you."

He threw down his hat and draped his jacket over his chair. "What'd he want?"

"Nothing important. Asked about the library vic."

"And what'd you tell him?" Toddle picked up a paper cup, popped the lid and sniffed. He grimaced and put it back.

"Told him I think we have another serial on our hands."

Wilkinson walked into the bullpen with the witness and a middle-aged man carrying a large sketchpad. Wolfe watched him head for his desk by the windows.

"But there's only been two bodies," Toddle said, pulling him back into the conversation. "It only becomes a serial after three."

"There's only two we've *found*. I put any money on that there's more out there. The way they're killed, the eye removal, the slashed neck, the staging of the bodies; it isn't some random jackass." Wolfe cracked his neck. Frustration boiled inside him.

Calm down.

He took a deep breath, exhaled.

"Look, everything points to a serial killer, even if we've only found two bodies. Trust me. There will be more. Assholes like this don't stop at two. They keep going until they get too old or caught or die."

"But two serial killers at the same time, in the same city?"

"In Long Island, between '89 and '93, there were *three* happening at once, and I remember growing up and seeing on the news that Vegas had the Hillside Strangler and the Freeway Killer at the same time, too."

"I remember that." He reclined, and rubbed his face. "They all ended up getting caught. I fucking hope ours don't end up like the Zodiac or Jack the Ripper."

Wolfe waved his hand in front of his nose. "They were lucky. Jack happened in the 1800s. If he was around today, his ass would've got caught early on. And, the Zodiac happened before DNA testing."

Toddle grabbed a pen. "I guess."

Wolfe picked up his desk phone and called for the lab reports on Timara Davis.

The morgue had agreed to take more work from other jurisdictions so they could prioritize the SSK victims. It wasn't only the police force feeling the pressure from the media. From how Wolfe understood it, their lab was getting all the grunt work. It helped that it was a teaching morgue, and Martin had a handful of up-and-comers under his wing.

Yet despite knowing the lead examiner, Wolfe's reach didn't go far. An assistant told him he'd get the reports tomorrow afternoon, maybe morning, but nothing before that. Wolf slammed the phone back into the cradle.

His cell phone went off and, without looking who it was, he answered.

"What?" he barked.

"Whoa, calm down."

Shit.

"Sorry, Cindy." He ran his hand through his hair. "What's going on?"

"Bad day?"

"Something like that."

"Anything I can do?"

"Unless you're a medical examiner, no."

She laughed. "Sorry to call you during work, I know you're busy, but I was wondering if you could try to get the weekend of the 28th off?"

He closed his eyes. With the possibility that SSK would strike again, or even that more women without eyes would appear, Wolfe couldn't just take a few days off. She probably wanted to stay at her grandparents' cabin for the weekend or take Tabby to the museum. He loved them both, but the amount of work piling up outweighed whatever ideas Cindy had planned.

"Probably not, but I could ask. Why?"

He thought he heard her whisper something, then she said: "It's Tabby's birthday."

Her voice faded away as if water filled his ears. Wolfe had forgotten his own daughter's birthday. Tabby's turning two wasn't even a blip on his radar. Cold washed over him and settled in his gut. He put his arm on his desk and rested his head on it. It had already been a year, and he couldn't remember anything between her first and second birthday.

How many times did I see her in a year?

Twenty, forty, sixty times total? And how many were those only in the morning before he left, or when he came home after she had already gone to bed? Had he taken her to the park this year? Had he been around to help her learn to walk or say her first words? Did she know who he was?

"Cindy?"

"What?"

"I'll get off that weekend."

"Really? I know your busy..."

"Doesn't matter." He smiled, imagining her birthday weekend. Opening her presents, eating cake with her name on it, spilling ice cream on the carpet. Briefly the murders, work, the station; none of it was important anymore. "I promise."

He heard her smile as she said, "Tabby will be *so* happy, Gary."

"Me too. I have to go. Tell Tabby I love her."

"I will. Love you."

"You too."

William Acerieas

HE SAT CROSSED-LEGGED ON the study floor, his back against the cellar door, the Family Book open in his lap. He started from the back of the book, where the Family Logs were kept since Lawrence Acerieas began them in 1785. Most entries were short, written in old English instead of the forgotten language. It wasn't until 1814 when James Acerieas II started using it to keep the Family's work hidden in plain view. The forgotten language had been around since the dawn of the written word, according to James, so some entries prior to 1814 had inklings of it throughout. Despite this, some resorted back to English for whatever reason.

None covered what he was looking for.

As William skimmed through the Family Book, he discovered no one spoke on the possibility that someone's quality of life could result in a higher quality Offering. Pages of details of his ancestors' own Offerings, gathered in villages and hamlets, in seedy alleys. Details on how they were stored in jars of formaldehyde procured from local morgues. Some even gave minute details on how to pickle them with jams, or how to properly hide them beneath floorboards or behind bookshelves.

William groaned. None scientifically explained if an unwed mother was the same as a married one or a widow, none gave conversions ratios for a virgin compared to a deflowered woman. A dull throb began in his temples. Sweat gathered under his arms.

I know I read it somewhere.

He skipped to 1861, running a finger down the lines until he got to Dr. Gregory Acerieas.

The name clicked into place. Now he remembered reading his works maybe ten years ago in one of the endless studies his grandfather oversaw. There were several long entries, all written in small, fine print.

I'm going to be here for a while.

He stood, stretched his back, and plodded into the kitchen. He left the Book on the table and started a pot of coffee. He made a sandwich, while the coffee percolated, and ate it, before grabbing a pad and pencil from the drawer by the backdoor. Evening settled in and golden light bled into the room.

William sat still and quiet, enjoying the brief reprieve before digging in, coffee at the ready. The cinnamon aroma complimented the darkening light perfectly. A minute later, he leaned over the Book.

He had to make a second pot to keep going and, yawning, he read his notes back, translated from the forgotten language to plain English.

Gregory only theorized what William sought after. Technology in 1861 either wasn't sufficient or was too expensive to test his hypothesis.

"Our ancestors have written theories of their own, and some have tried to no avail. All can be read in the Logs. I believe they did not have a background in the field of science, since most formulas and equations made little sense, or they did not understand the foundation of the Offerings, resulting in many mistakes.

*"Thus, I have come to the conclusion that logic reigns supreme when dealing with Offerings, that the infallible intelligence of reasoning works the same as ours in the Other Place. It is to be followed: A woman with child provides more energy, more—what I now consider—*Unseen Strength, *compared to a fertile, yet not deflowered, woman.*

"However, I am unable to prove this. The results of Offerings are invisible to us here in this world, but I believe that there is a higher degree of chance that the connection would be created through the use of mother and child instead of a woman without child, especially if fresh.

"Furthermore, my belief is that an infant is the strongest of an Offering, attributing to the innocence of a child's mind, and its unblemished eyes. They see the world far differently than adults do, and thus that abstract, powerful, childish wonder, brims with Unseen Strength.*"*

"Unseen Strength," William said, running his palm down his face. "Unseen Strength." He'd never heard the energy of an Offering spoken in such a way, even by his grandfather. He had always said it was like wind but stronger, immeasurable by this world. Always present but never seen or felt, only in the Other.

It made as much sense now as it did then. *How could this world measure something meant for the Other? Physics would be different there; science would be fundamentally abnormal compared to here.*

Yet with the use of Unseen Strength, he could create the connection between both worlds. Many before him had futilely sacrificed their earthly bodies for the cause, but William felt deep in his bones that he would be the one to make it happen, now knowing Dr. Gregory's theory.

What if you end up like them? Like father, mother? Failing everyone who've you ever loved, the ones most important to you. All those years of studying, years of them and no one else, numberless hours reading, learning, becoming who the Family needed. All those people killed for nothing.

He gripped the table. "It's the only way."

What will you do if the results are just your consciousness transferring to the Other? No connection, no bridge. And if you're successful, then what? No one's remained to make the passage yet. Either path is for nothing, the Family ending with you.

"No. Not for nothing. Never for nothing." His breath was heavy and he felt tears coming. "It gives them a chance to return. I will tell them there that their new bodies can pass through. I will return again, too."

Will you?

Or will you become like your parents?

His father sat in the chair in the workshop. His wrists, ankles, and neck were strapped down. The copper helmet covered his brown hair, and the circular discs blocked his matching eyes. His grandfather roved around the cellar, making sure there were no kinks in the wiring. William, freshly turned 6-years-old, stood in the red brick doorway. His sweaty hands gripped the rough surface. His father smiled, and his mother kissed him before standing by the wall, crossing her arms. His father stared in William's general direction and mouthed, "I love you."

His grandfather pulled the lever.

Although he couldn't possibly understand what happened, his grandfather explained it to him a year later. When the lever was pulled, holes opened in the black discs and allowed the Offering-fueled substance to drain into the helmet's tubing. Razor sharp prongs in the eye-covers pierced the eye sockets, avoiding the eyes, and injected the fluid directly into the brain.

Then white light filled the cellar. Sounds of boiling oceans and tearing metal flooded the air, and it felt like a giant smacked William across his entire body. He crashed onto the floor and cracked his head. He tried to ignore the pain and rubbed the burning from his eyes. It went on for seconds, but if felt like hours. Then, the light faded and the noise quietened and the room returned to normal. He could feel the silence, not hear it, because an incessant ringing droned in his ears.

Slowly William got to his feet. His father was slumped in his chair. His flesh was waxy and pale, his mouth agape and bright red. Nothing occupied the space above the Family Crest in the ground. No portal. No connection. No bridge.

It was impossible. Even when dozens of the family had failed, his father could do it, he could do practically anything...

When his mother screamed, he heard it. Frozen, dumbstruck, watching his grandfather undo the straps and remove the helmet to reveal brittle white hair, hollowed cheeks, protruding bone, and pearly eyes.

William raked his teeth over his lower lip while tears fell. He didn't want to remember anymore. Didn't want to relive the loss, the pain, the hurt. He wished it would end. He wished he knew why his mind was barreling through the past. He was doing what he's been told from the beginning. Why disrupt that?

The memory of his father dissipated and his mother emerged in the same chair.

Two weeks later. The soil of his father's grave still unsettled, his grandfather insisted his mother take her turn. He said there was enough remaining in the vats for one more use. It didn't take much for his mother to agree. Although she never said it out loud, William believed she thought her love would create a stronger bond, and bring them back together.

That night, after he was picked up from the library, his mother was strapped into the chair. His hands were small fists, and tears and snot dribbled down his face. He understood but didn't like it. His grandfather stood by his side, his fingers digging into his shoulder, his other hand holding the lever.

"I love you, Willy," she said, lips trembling.

"Love you, too," he said.

The switch was thrown.

Blinding white light; tearing metal, boiling seas. His grandfather kept him on his feet against the pressure that knocked him back before.

The lights dimmed and the high-pitch whining was in his ears again.

No connection.

Failed.

William didn't stay to watch her be unstrapped. Sprinting upstairs to his bedroom on the second story he slammed the door shut and collapsed onto his bed.

It wasn't until his grandfather opened his door the next morning that he realized he'd been in the room all day. His grandfather told him that his mother's burial was tomorrow, and to be dressed and ready. William didn't answer.

It was only the two of them then, but his grandfather's health was unknowingly waning, the undiagnosed lung cancer already working through him. All those years of smoking finally took their toll. He stopped actively participating in the Family's work to focus on William's studies more than before. His importance grew. He must be the one to build the bridge, the one to complete the journey that so many before him failed.

The only interactions with outside the Family was the library, and he was promptly pulled from there. No friends, no hopes or thoughts of significant others, nor children. His entire purpose was nothing but an effigy for the Family, commonalities of average life foreign to him.

Studies and history morning and night. Learning how to harvest without being discovered, how to store them properly in the jars, and how to use them once the time came. The vats and how they were worked. The chair's straps and helmet. However, nothing touched on the After besides the potential godly shapes they'd become, nothing about what the connection may look like.

What would happen if he succeeded? He didn't ponder it too much, because surely his grandfather would be there to instruct him on what to do when it happened.

Heart pounding in his chest, he splayed his fingers across the table. Him failing would mean the entire Family failed. With Dr. Gregory's information, he believed he could make it work. A mother. An infant. By using them, he was certain the connection would be made. His mother, father, everyone before him, would find their way back in the incomprehensible bodies they had desperately fought for.

They will welcome me with open arms. Praise me. Reward me. Love me. And this world will bow before us.

All because of me.

MARCH 14, 1994

Detective Wolfe

WOLFE GOT TAMIRA DAVIS's lab reports a little after lunch.

Her eyes were removed in the same way that Susan's had been, although not as cleanly. Large portions of the optic nerves remained in the sockets, some shredded, others crudely torn, which led Andriana Mudwood, the ME, to believe the eyes were forced out instead of severed, pulled or roughly removed by a tool. Her time of death was put at around 1AM.

All the blood at the scene was from the victim, none from the killer. A trace amount of caffeine was in her system. No other substances or alcohol. No semen, lubricant, or other evidence of penetration had been found.

Wolfe noted the lack of drugs and turned the page.

Like the first victim, the cut through her neck had been what killed her, leading to asphyxiation and blood loss. She suggested the weapon might have been a medical tool, such as a scalpel. The slice ran from the right external jugular vein, the sternomastoid muscle, then the right common carotid artery, coming out through the opposite side.

Wait a second.

He pulled out his notes from Susan's murder.

...cut through the left...

...left common carotid...

In his own handwriting, circled: *Killer is right-handed.*

Did she make a mistake?

He picked up the phone and called the lab.

Wolfe was surprised to hear Martin on the other side. Typically, his underlings answered the phones.

"For Tamira Davis, was her report accurate?"

"Hold on. Adriana, my new assistant, did them. Lemme check..." Wolfe heard shuffling of papers, moving folders and files. "Yeah, looks about right."

"Are you sure, Martin?"

His became stern. "We might be overworked but I approve the reports myself before they're sent over."

Are there two killers?

A copycat? Doubtful. There was no media coverage besides an obit in the papers on the first vic.

He wrote the information down, and, glancing at the papers, realized what was missing from the report, what he had forgotten.

"Was there a brand found?"

"I... what?"

"A brand. A similar victim had a brand."

"Like a tattoo?"

Wolfe rubbed his forehead. "Yes, like a tattoo, but burned onto the skin. Would've looked like a hexagon with lines inside."

He heard Martin flip through pages.

"Yeah, there was a tattoo like that on her left forearm."

No fucking mistakes, huh?

Wolfe let out warm breath. "Can you fax over everything you have on it?"

"Yeah, sure."

The detective hung up.

Ten minutes later he received the fax. The 'tattoo' on Tamira's forearm matched Susan's. Same geometrical shape, same internal lines, same everything except Tamira's was sloppier, as though the killer ran out of time.

Probably when he heard the witness coming,

He jotted down the new information in his pad. Wolfe yawned as Toddle came into the station carrying four coffees and brown paper bag smelling of cinnamon sugar. A folder was pinched under his arm. "Look what daddy brought."

"You're a lifesaver."

Toddle set everything down on his desk and brought over a coffee and cinnamon roll. He held out the file. "Want to know something even better than this?"

Wolfe opened the lid on the cup and inhaled the rich smell of fresh coffee. "What?"

"I did my own digging on Tamira Davis." He opened the file. "She was a 68-year-old grandmother and wife, and lived in an apartment on the upper north side, alone."

"Where's the husband?"

"Griseo Estates, a nursing home a couple miles from her apartment. I was going to give them a call now then go up and talk to him. Her kids live outside the city, but they'll be there, too. I also have a copy of this." Toddle gave Wolfe the killer's composite.

The man was younger than he expected, maybe early-to-mid-twenties. Dark hair wafted over a protruding brow; his eyes deep-seated as if he didn't sleep much. He had sunken cheeks, and a small, narrow chin under thin lips.

"This is the guy?"

"That's what the witness says."

"Looks like a fish."

Toddle laughed. "I guess he does, if you look at it from an angle."

Wolfe put the sketch in Tamira's file. "Do you need help talking to her family?"

"Don't worry about it, just enjoy your coffee. You already did the deskwork. Just don't get too smitten by that guy's stare."

"Can I borrow that file for a few minutes to copy some of it?"

"No problem, gives me a little extra time to relax."

"Thanks."

The detective began quickly writing. The coffee and cinnamon went cold, forgotten.

MARCH 28, 1994

Detective Wolfe

THE SUN STREAMING THROUGH the window filled their bedroom with soft morning light. Wolfe groaned as he rolled over. He smelled Cindy's hair, lavender, spilling onto his side of the bed. He smiled and settled back into sleep. It was Friday. He had requested the time off and, surprisingly, got it, although he agreed to cover some shifts to compensate. More paperwork was coming his way, but at that moment he didn't care.

Drifting back towards unconsciousness, Susan Tanaka and Tamira Davis came to him. There were connections, no doubt about it, and Wolfe was certain it was the same killer, except for one major flaw. Tanaka was killed left to right, while Davis was murdered right to left. The killer could've been ambidextrous, but after searching on Netscape, he found that it was extremely rare. They could've learned to use both hands effectively, but why would someone do that? He had a gut feeling that wasn't the case.

Also...

He forced his thoughts away and focused on his wife sleeping next to him. Again, he dipped his toes into the waters of slumber, and was about to take the plunge when his phone rang.

Shit.

"Don't answer it," Cindy said, half-asleep. She rolled over and draped her arm across him. He opened his eyes, meeting the crisp blue eyes he fell in love with locked onto him. "Don't answer it."

"What if…"

She put a finger to his mouth, then pressed her lips to his ear. "Don't answer it.".

A chill ran down his spine. He shivered as she coiled her arm around his back and pulled him onto her side of the bed. She took his hand and guided his fingers to her groin.

The phone stopped ringing.

His fingers rested on the crotch of her panties. Her warmth radiated through the thin fabric. He pulled them aside and, finding her already wet, gently entered her.

"Now aren't you glad you didn't answer?" She grinned.

He sat on the edge of the bed, listening to the shower run. His groin throbbed with a pleasurable soreness.

Been a while, hasn't it?

His attention turned from the open bathroom door to his cell phone.

Two calls and five texts from Toddle.

One call from the Captain. He played the voicemail.

"Wolfe, you better pick up. I don't give a shit if you're in Europe frolicking in a field of flowers, when I call, you pick up. SSK got another one. Lower west side, Motel 42 on Spring Drive. When you hear this, get there."

He set the phone onto the bed and rubbed his face.

They had Tabby's birthday party this evening, just the three of them. Tomorrow, they planned on going to the park and the museum with his parents, and on Sunday they were having lunch with Cindy's parents.

If he left now he could be back before the party, like he never left. Toddle could've done most of the legwork by the time he got there, or so he hoped. It'd be open and shut. Go in, do the usual, and leave.

Wolfe dressed quickly and rushed to the bathroom. Cindy was still in the shower, humming some upbeat, quirky song he didn't know.

"Cind?" he called over the water.

She stopped humming. "Yeah?"

His stomach churned and his hands and face were cold.

"The Captain called. There's been another SSK hit."

Silence.

"I'm just going to run in, do what I have to, and come home."

Silence.

"I'll be back before tonight. I promise I won't do anything work related after I'm back."

"You promised about today, too."

Wolfe opened his mouth to speak, but nothing came out. The only sound was the running water.

"Honey…" he started, but Cindy cut him off.

"Just go, just fucking go. You better be at her party tonight, or so help me God, Gary…"

"I will be. I won't miss it, I promise." He turned and went for the bedroom door but caught himself and turned back. "I love you!"

She didn't reply.

After plowing through the mob of journalists out front, mold slapped Wolfe in the face when he entered Motel 42. It tasted of decay. Past cops talking to a tall man with hollow eyes who he assumed was the owner, he took the stairs two at a time.

Toddle had said it was room B10, second level. Two officers stood outside the taped-off room. Wolfe flashed his badge and went in.

Toddle looked up from his notepad. "Look who finally joined us on this beautiful morning."

Toddle and the Captain were on the far side of the room. Past them, in the closet-sized bathroom, was the woman in the tub. A blue tie with white stripes bound her wrists to the spigot. Wet blonde hair slicked back. Mouth open. Bloated tongue hanging over her bottom lip. A cut ran across her throat and blood had spilled down her chest. Her breasts tightly bound in brown belts.

The Captain came up behind him. "Definitely SSK."

"Do we have anything yet?"

"They've already taken photographs, and samples of the victim's blood, fibers on the bed, floor, dusted for prints, the whole works. They're probably already back at the lab." Captain Conti turned to him. "Why are you rushing?"

"I'm off today."

He pointed to the bathroom. "I'll make sure she apologizes."

"If," he said through gritted teeth, "everything's already done, what was the point of calling me in?"

"I don't know, *Gary*, to do your *damn* job? Toddle can't do everything. Look around, Detective. Inspect something. Do anything that may help catch this bastard." He left the room without giving Wolfe a chance to reply.

Wolfe snatched a pair of latex gloves from the box on the dresser and returned to the bathroom. His temples throbbed and the base of his neck started to ache. His tongue was pressed to the roof of his mouth. Kneeling in front of the body and pulling on the gloves, he searched for anything different to the previous SSK murders. No scratches or bruises on the skin on the front. Hair was clean, with no dandruff or greasiness. Limbs were unblemished, and both her fingernails and toenails were cut. If they had skin particles from the killer beneath them from a struggle, they were long gone. Wolfe turned her over and found her back and rear as clean as the front. Besides the toothbrush particles they'd likely find, her groin was clean, too.

As he peered into the drain, his mind wandered back to Susan Tanaka and Tamira Davis. He knew he should want to get home but when he was working, he couldn't think about anything else, like slipping into a different version of himself. Work-Wolfe.

Shaking his head to clear his thoughts, he refocused on the scene before him. Nothing was in the drain, the faucet, or the showerhead. Everything was wiped down. It reeked of bleach. The bottles of shampoo and soap were gone, which wasn't new. SSK was meticulous, much like Susan's killer. Not a trace of anything or anyone from SSK... *He messed up with Tamira, though, because there was a lot more blood, whoever did her in was acting fast and they had a witness...*

Wolfe stood and wiped his forehead with his wrist. The sink, mirror, walls, and ceiling were spotless. He lifted the toilet tank lid to find only water. Like all the others. Time wasted, like he anticipated. Wolfe cared for the poor woman, but he knew he wasn't being productive here. The only way SSK was going to be caught was if he made a mistake, simple as that. From the looks of it, he didn't fuck up here.

He removed the gloves and left the bathroom.

Toddle stopped rummaging through a nightstand. "Where're you going?"

"To the station."

"For what?"

"If Conti wants me to do my job, then I'm going to go work on something I can actually make headway on."

Frustration faded on the drive to the station. Being alone and the automatic, almost instinctive, action of steering the car down the road was like meditation. With the sound of the engine and the ticking of the turn signal, he could easily lose himself in the motions. If he hadn't become a detective, he imagined he would've been a taxi driver or delivery man. Medial, boring work, but soothing and mindless, nonetheless. By the time he was behind his desk he was calm, clear-headed, and ready to dive back into the case.

Two full pages of detailed handwritten notes comparing the Susan Tanaka and Tamira Davis cases sat in front of him. Both had their eyes removed, skin branded, and throats slashed. They were both women and had been killed in public places.

That's where the similarities ended.

Tamira was 72-years-old, a grandmother, a retired librarian, and lived in the city; Susan was 21-years-old, a college student, and she didn't live in Cherry Brooke outside of college. Tamira was murdered by a right-handed man, while Tamira, assuming the killer wasn't ambidextrous, was killed by a left-handed man. Susan was found with high levels of procaine and benzodiazepine in her system, but Tamira was not.

He didn't have time to follow up with every lead, but through brief phone calls, background checks, and Netscape searches, Wolfe concluded that whoever the killer was, they probably weren't connected to the victims personally.

Susan's parents lived in Mistvale and were home when the murder occurred. Neither had a criminal record and both had alibi. Added to that, he couldn't imagine those nice folks going all that way to murder a daughter whose death crushed them that day at the morgue. She had no boyfriend, something confirmed by her parents and what little friends she had back home. The few at the University couldn't have killed a spider if they wanted to.

Tamira's three children were all married and at home asleep at the time of her murder. Her husband was wheelchair bound. Her grandchildren were in their late teens, and all lived a few hours outside the city. All had good alibis. After running their names in the police database, their records were spotless.

Further confirming his suspicions, none of the victims' families looked anything like the sketch of the suspect from the Davis murder.

The victims didn't know each other. No connections. They were complete strangers.

Wolfe sighed.

There was still enough to go on, however. There was the same MO, same ritualistic positions of the bodies, the cut throats, the eyewitness and the composite. They weren't sexual crimes. Wolfe assumed that Susan hadn't been his first because of how clean her death had been, and Tamira's likely would've been the same if it had not been interrupted.

Captain Conti opened his office door. Wolfe grabbed his files and met him at the doorway.

"Can I speak to you for a minute, Cap?"

"You're supposed to be across town."

"He didn't need me," Wolfe said as he forced himself into his office. It smelled of smoke and alcohol. A small desk in the center was flanked by two filing cabinets. Red lights blinked on his phone. The lower drawer of the right cabinet was partially open, and a bottle glinted under the overhead lights. Black and white photographs hung along the wood-paneled walls: the Captain with the commander and the mayor, him at an awards ceremony, his wedding day. Two chairs faced the desk.

Conti shut the door. "Sorry about the outburst earlier, I know it's your day off."

"No problem." *Make me work on the only days I requested off in years. Fucking asshole.*

His boss sunk into the chair behind the desk, snatched a pack of cigarrettes and pulled one out with pinched lips. "So, what do you want?"

He set the two opened files face-up on his desk, then his notes. He didn't know what to do with his hands, so he shoved them in his pockets. "I think we've got another serial killer."

He glanced at the papers, then back up at Wolfe. "You sure?"

He nodded. "Skim through those and tell me what you think."

Holding the smoldering cigarette in his mouth, picking up the files, he leaned back and read. Ten minutes later with a fresh smoke between his fingers, Conti looked up and shook his head. "There're definitely some similarities, but there's only two cases, and possibly being two different people, we just don't have the manpower or money right now."

For a second Wolfe forgot to breathe, and he inhaled. He stabbed the pages with his finger. "Captain, there's so many similarities. The removal of the eyes, their throats, the way the bodies are positioned, both in public places..."

The Captain's eyes thinned. "Wolfe, you think I can't read?"

Wolfe shook his head.

"Then don't point out the fucking obvious." Splotches of red rose in his cheeks. "I see the same shit as you, but we can't look into this now with SSK going on." He held his cigarette and threw his free hand towards the wall. "Outside this place is a shit-show and we're the ones who have to put it back together with tape and glue. It hardly holds it together and it breaks fast, but we get on our damn knees, pick up the pieces, and put it back together again, over and over."

He slammed his palms onto the desk. Ash spilled over Wolfe's work. "Trust me when I say I want to see this bastard behind bars. Hell, if I could, I'd tell you to drop everything and go work on this, but the world doesn't stop spinning when there's a killer on the loose. There could be two dozen other psychopaths out there we don't know about, and I try not think about how much shit we're missing because we're focused on one asshole." He sighed. "We don't have the resources to do everything, Gary. We go after the biggest fish first."

"But, what about their families?" Wolfe's frustration got the better of him. "Tamira's kids? Susan's parents?"

"Wolfe..."

"What if they went to the papers?" he continued, knowingly crossing the line. "What if the media starts putting pressure on us to find *this* killer? What then? Are these women going to keep dying until one of them is rich or famous or white?"

Conti rose from his seat, his face beat-red. "Don't you fucking dare question my integrity, Gary! Don't you dare imply this is racial." He pointed to the door. "Get the hell out and don't show your face until you have something on an actual killer!"

Wolfe grabbed his files and stormed out the office, leaving the door open. He heard the whine of wheels moving, the clink of glass on wood, then the Captain's door slam shut.

Wolfe dropped everything on his desk and dropped in his chair. He surged with adrenaline, fear, anxiety. He took a deep breath and closed his eyes. Exhaled, stretched out his fingers over the armrest. He was lucky he hadn't been fired; lucky he hadn't decked him for his remarks. Not every day you can tell your boss he's racist and walk away scot-free.

The adrenaline ebbed away and soon he was shaking. He stared at the mildew-spotted tiled ceiling.

Now what? I could go to the media, maybe force Conti to do something but I'd lose my job, and we can't survive on only Cindy's pay.

After a few moments, a new thought. *Maybe the lab missed something else?*

"Wouldn't be the first time." He picked up the phone.

"Hello?" A woman's voice.

"Is Martin around?"

"Hold on."

"What's up?" Martin said.

"Do you remember the Tamira Davis case?"

"Adriana did the report, right? What about it?"

Toddle came into the station. He looked rundown. Beat. Their tired eyes met briefly before quickly breaking.

"Was there anything she found not included in the report?"

It went silent on the other end. "Are you insinuating something again, Wolfe?"

"No, nothing like that." Wolfe watched Toddle sink into his chair and throw his hat onto the desktop. "Just maybe there was something not important enough to mention, something that wasn't worth the ink on the paper."

"That screwed, huh?" Martin said.

"To the moon and back."

"I can personally review it, if you want, we still have the body until the kids come on Monday, but it'll cost you."

Wolfe groaned. "How much?"

"Let's just say you have an I.O.U indebted to me, and I can redeem it whenever I want."

"You know bribing a cop is illegal?"

"Do you want me to look or not?"

"Fine, whatever. I.O.U it is. When can I hear back from you?"

"Give me a couple hours, I'll call your cell with the results."

The line went dead.

Before leaving the station, Wolfe went to Toddle's desk. He skimmed the notes his partner worked on. He'd got nothing from the scene, either. Wolfe patted him on the back and gave him a fiver for coffee and a doughnut from the cafe down the street. They didn't speak, but Wolfe figured the Lincoln was his way of apologizing for earlier without saying it.

He parked in his driveway, turned off the car, and ran up the porch.

Pink and white streamers dangled from the living room ceiling, balloons stuck in the corners, some scattered on the carpet. He weaved around the recliner to the coffee table where Cindy sat with Tabby in her lap. Cindy's frizzy hair was tied back, and Tabby's brunette bangs were tucked behind her ears. A small cake with pink and white icing was on the table, and written in red syrup on the top was '*Happy 2nd Birthday Tabby!*' Two candles stuck out from either side of the lettering.

"Glad you could make it," Cindy said as he sat across from her. Wolfe could tell her smile was forced.

"Yeah, sorry." He leaned over the table and kissed Tabby's forehead. "Happy birthday, little girl."

Tabby smiled, but her eyes remained on the cake.

"I think she wants that more than us right now," Wolfe said, laughing.

"Maybe."

Wolfe found a lighter in his pockets and lit the candles. He reached over and flicked off the lights. Candlelight bathed the Wolfe family in a soft, warm glow, casting faint shadows on the walls.

Cindy's and Tabby's eyes glistened. Wolfe's chest hitched and a chill trickled down his back as he blinked back tears. He smiled, then began 'Happy Birthday.' Cindy joined in, swaying, Tabby on her lap. When the song ended, Cindy whispered into her daughter's ear, "Now make a wish and blow out the candles."

His daughter puckered her mouth and blew, sending spittle flying onto the cake. She blew and blew until one candle died with a hiss, then focused her efforts onto the other one, but it wouldn't give under her breath. Wolfe let out a quick puff and the candle extinguished. Tabby fell back against her mother, clapping and squealing.

"Good job, Tabby!" Cindy glanced across at Wolfe, who got up and threw on the lights. "I'll go get a knife."

As he was pulling out plates from the cabinet his phone went off. He set them down on the counter and answered. "Yeah?" He glanced down the hall. If Cindy knew he was taking a work call, he'd be in even deeper shit.

"It's Martin."

"What's up?" He took out three forks, then put one back. Cindy would feed Tabby.

"I reviewed everything."

"And?" He ripped off some paper towels and put them on the plates. Grabbed a knife from the block.

"I'm not saying Adriana made a mistake, she's new, but I've got something she might have thought was so insignificant, what with missing eyes and all, she didn't include it in the report."

"Just tell me what it is."

"Dry cement. I tested it myself. There were particles of it on her clothes—her body was clean when it came in, I double-checked. It was on the surface of the fibers. Other dirt in the clothes is so baked in that the cement stands out like a sore thumb. It's fresh, premixed most likely, probably from whoever killed her."

Wolfe put the forks with the paper towels. "Thanks Martin. I'll call you back."

"Wait, don't tell anyone about this, Adriana could..."

Wolfe hung up, tossed the phone onto the counter, and returned to the living room.

Cindy eyed him. "Took you long enough."

He set a plate, fork, and paper towel in front of her, then grabbed a set for himself. "Yeah, well, I move slow. Sue me."

After about half of the cake was eaten, Tabby's portion smashed, played with, and cleaned from her face, they gave her the presents. Stuffed animals, puzzles, a coloring book, and a box of crayons soon littered the floor. Tabby played with whatever was closest and watched *The Lion King* until bedtime.

Cindy carried her upstairs into the bathroom while Wolfe cleaned up downstairs, after which he trudged up into the bedroom and got into bed. He listened to Cindy leave the bathroom and take Tabby into her room, speak softly to their daughter, then the light switch click. She came into their room and stared at Wolfe accusingly like he was a child caught by his mother, but then the expression passed and she went into the bathroom.

She came out from the bathroom in her nightgown and got into bed, her back to him. She switched off the lamp, and silence, like night itself, settled over them.

Wolfe wanted to say something to break the awkwardness. She was still mad about him leaving earlier, clearly, even though he got home before the party. He didn't want to argue before bed either, or before their day out tomorrow, but...

He groaned as he rolled away, facing the wall.

Better that we don't talk. Maybe she'll calm down by the morning.

The next day he woke to an empty bed. Tabby and Cindy were downstairs already in the kitchen, his wife frying eggs and Tabby at the table, coloring. Cindy glared at him across the room and it felt like she stared straight into Wolfe's soul.

Great.

APRIL 6, 1994

William Acerieas

FRIGID WIND HOWLED AROUND the creaking house. Snow clogged the frosted window above the sink. William pulled his coat tighter over him and read the gas bill in his free hand.

Late Notice

He skipped to the bottom.

Amount Due: $184.00

Late Fee: $30.00

Total Due: $214.00

Grumbling, he set the bill down with the others.

Electric.

Gas.

Water.

Sewage.

No phone, thankfully. His grandfather had abandoned the landline two years ago in favor of a cell phone from the '80s. He was worried someone would listen in on his calls and put their work in danger.

The inheritance had only lasted a few months, and now it was nearly empty, there was not enough to pay the bills.

Maybe he thought I would've used the machine by now?

It was possible that William had mismanaged the funds, but how could he have known? Grandfather never taught him about paying bills, budgeting, being financially responsible. He had been homeschooled, and had assumed things were taken care of automatically like when he was a child. No one prepared him for life beyond the Family. It was only his father who taught him how to drive, and who pushed him to get his license. Will figured it was because he'd need the skill later.

He stared at the pile of bills on the table.

All of this was alien to him as dating or making friends. All he knew was the Family's work, history, philosophies. Everything else hadn't been in his grandfather's curriculum. William assumed he'd made certain his grandson would be fine his own for the rest of his life and not have to worry about money by saving enough, but guess not.

His stomach grumbled. Upon opening the fridge, he found a box of baking soda in the back and a head of pinking lettuce in the crisper. Checking the cabinet, he checked the coffee can and found it empty. A shrill whistling came through a draft somewhere in the house.

I need money, but I can't work.

I have the Family's work.

Maybe...

William went upstairs. There were two bedrooms, the restroom, and the attic. He winced as cold air wafted over him as he opened the attic door, and ascended the tight, winding stairs. The floor was finished, but the ceiling was not. Pink, cloudy insulation bulged from between the rafters.

Where do I start?

From one end of the room to the other were the things his grandfather had collected over the decades: mahogany and redwood dressers, nightstands, chairs, tall antique lamps with Victorian lampshades, stacks of leather-bound books caked in dust, a faded pink and blue rocking horse against the far wall sitting next to a rusted metal boxcar, a small satchel of broken bird whistles, and other toys from his grandfather's childhood.

William was never instructed what to do with them. They were his grandfather's, and even though he was gone, a pang of guilt came with considering selling the lot. He picked at his bottom lip as he took in the room again. They weren't his, per se... Wind rattled the window.

I need the money. I can't complete my task without it.

After deciding what could and couldn't be let go of, he returned to the kitchen and picked up the phone. He flipped to the Bargain Bulletin in the newspaper and called the number.

An old woman answered him, and he quickly rattled off what he wanted to sell, and their prices. He agreed to leave all the items in the paper until they were sold.

He hung up and sat in a chair. His stomach grumbled again. As he kneaded his abdomen, a dull throb began behind his eyes.

William exhaled through clenched teeth and rubbed the space between his brows.

I would do anything for food and a coffee.

April 15, 1994

William Acerieas

"Next!"

He shuffled forward, halting before he ran into the man in front of him. He pulled his collar tighter. He'd come to know the yellowed tiled ceiling and chipped floor of the church's basement well in the last week or so. The stench of sweat, mildew, and other bodily odors was almost overpowering. The man before him wore a tattered green blanket that hung loosely over his thin frame, the hem dragging on the linoleum. William was careful to not step on it. Who knew what the man would do if he did?

At end of the line, someone asked, "Hey, hey, do you have a qwuater?"

"Next!"

Another step forward. *Not too close.*

A TV sat on a metal mount in the corner of the room. It was muted with closed captions on, which he read as he moved absently along. A female reporter stood in front of a dilapidated hotel. Cops went in and out, journalists pushing against the barriers flanking the entrance.

"Just hours ago, there was another murder by the South Side Killer." The lady turned and the camera zoomed in on the brown brick building. *"Only a few yards away, in one of those rooms, a young woman was going about her day when he attacked."* The camera zoomed out to focus back on the newscaster. A tall, bulky detective with his hands shoved in his coat pockets came out the door. Behind him, EMTs brought out a gurney covered in a white sheet between them. *"Police have stated they're working tirelessly on catching the SSK, but it's clear to the terrified citizens of Cherry Brooke that they aren't doing enough to temper their fears. I hope, pray, that he's in custody soon."*

William jumped at the sound of metal hitting metal. An unwashed counter ran the length of the fogged, empty display cases. A Styrofoam tray carrying gold and cup of coffee were already waiting for him to take. Behind the counter, the woman glared at him. He took the tray and hurried to a table.

He sat at the end of a long, stained table. At the other end was a mother and son in threadbare clothing, laughing to one another as they ate.

Ignoring the loss sinking into his gut, he ripped open the packet of saltines and crumbled them into what looked like tomato soup. He swirled it around with his plastic spoon. The smell alone made him hesitant, but this was one of his few meals for the next few days, so he took a spoonful and swallowed it.

Uck. Watery tomatoes.

As he ate, he pondered on what was left in the attic. Hardly anything had sold—*because it's junk or because it's winter?*—and what *did* sell hadn't helped much with the bills. Only the electricity and water remained on. The mortgage was unpaid, but he heard of people who did the same for months and kept their homes. He assumed the bank was slow with foreclosing, so he didn't worry too much about it yet. Soon he would harvest what he needed to and would no longer have to deal with any of those things anyway.

The next Offerings and the machine.

A tinge of fear danced down his spine. His stomach clenched.

Why am I so afraid?

Was it taking the steps his parents and others had taken and failed? Was it because the results were unknown once the lever was thrown? Was it due to his comfortability with the world, with his home? Everything he knew and possessed would be relinquished for something that neither he, nor anyone else, truly understood.

But the Book...

The Book stated so, but they were theories and hypotheses, beliefs founded on older beliefs going all the way back to its birth. The Other Place, the transmogrification of his body and the power therein, even the bridge itself—what exactly was it? Would it look the way the Book said? How would he know what to do once there?

More and more of the same rigmarole tumbled around in his skull until his head ached, and he wished more than ever for it all to stop and let him become what he's meant to become.

Become the conduit. Put myself into the chair and wear the helmet, then activate the machine with a rope tied to the lever. Needles digging into my eyes, the concoction flooding my brain. It can't feel good. It can't be pleasurable. It will be agony, pain I've never felt in my life.

Do I want that?

Fear bloomed like frozen wings over his back, enveloping the rest of him. His grip tightened on the plastic spoon in the empty bowl.

Does it have to be me?

Yes, it must be of our blood. Pure blood.

Who says?

Grandfather. The Book. My ancestors.

None of them are around. No one would know, and if it fails...

He could harvest more. It could be a test. A test that, if successful, would avoid all the physical pain of the process.

It would be easy.

Someone unimportant. Someone who doesn't matter. Someone who won't be missed.

Warmth billowed from his sternum and the dread dissipated. He drank the bitter coffee, now lukewarm. A smile crept over his face.

MAY 2, 1994

William Acerieas

"Yes, the dresser is still for sale. Absolutely. Yes. At four? That works for me. Thank you."

William hung up. That was the third call that day. He smiled to himself and got a glass of water.

"It was the weather." It seemed that soon after all the snow had melted and the sun came out, everyone decided to check the newspaper and seen his advertisement. He'd managed to sell most of the furniture and lamps, as well as a few old books and toys, although there were plenty left. He learned how to pay bills and manage money from some books at the church. If sales kept up, he'd be able to live comfortably for a few months, and have some savings left over.

As he put his empty glass down, the phone rang.

"Hello?"

"Hi, yes, is this William?"

He nodded as though the person could see. "Yes, that's me. Who is this?"

"My name's Cindy Wolfe. I just saw your ad in the paper, wish I would've seen it sooner, but was wondering if you still had the rocking horse for sale?"

He ran up into the attic to double-check it was there. "Yes, I still have it."

"How much are you asking for?"

"I believe the ad said somewhere around a hundred."

"Could you go any lower?" she said. "Sorry, just money's tight and—"

"How about seventy-five? It needs a new coat of paint and it's quite old, but still in great condition."

"That sounds great! When can I pick it up? Can we meet somewhere?"

"The 11th's good. I have other sales the day before, so I can't leave the house. How about outside the Cherry Brooke Museum?"

"Sorry, I'm working on the 11th and won't be able to get there until late, and I'll have my daughter with me; the horse is a late birthday present."

A mother, an infant.

His chest tightened as his heart rate skyrocketed.

Calm. Calm.

"That's okay, six works for me, or later if you need. I don't have other sales on that day. Also, your daughter won't be a problem. I'm good with children."

"Great! Outside the museum at around six on the 11th. Thank you so much. She'll love it. Have a good day."

"You too. Bye."

His fingers trembled as he hung up. He let the phone fall to the ground.

"A mother… a child…"

He walked backwards until his back was against the wall, and slid down to the floor. A prickly sensation flowed over his limbs into his chest, settled in his stomach for a while, and lapped his spine into the back of his head. He dug his fingertips into the floorboards.

"It's happening. It's happening."

Far too soon. Haven't settled on being the conduit…

…doesn't matter, does not matter, the time is now…

Just harvest the Offerings and figure the rest out after.

He got to his feet and went down into the cellar to prepare.

MAY 11, 1994

Detective Wolfe

WOLFE SAT IN THE station parking lot with the radio on.

"In other news, the South Side Killer has struck again yesterday. A young woman was found at the Cornerstone Motel on the lower north side. This is the SSK's sixth victim, and the police are no closer to catching this man than they were when the first was found."

He turned the car off and listened to the car slowly die. He set his forehead onto the steering wheel and closed his eyes.

The world made no sense. How could someone murder six people and not leave a trace of evidence? Was it someone working from inside the police system? Maybe a powerful government official? Was it a corrupt millionaire using his money to silence all the higher-ups and keep them quiet? He was a damn ghost. The detective couldn't wrap his mind around it.

More questions sprouted. Did the SSK do this elsewhere, or just here? Were there more bodies they hadn't found? Or had he moved from keeping the bodies in tubs to dumping them in the river and we're looking in the wrong place? It didn't match his MO and most killers didn't change, but the possibility remained.

He sighed.

With the murders, Wolfe was working more than ever before since Toddle had quit. Wolfe came in one morning and there was Toddle at his desk, wearing civilian clothes. His head was in his hand, boxes on the desk. People moved around him as though he had the plague.

"So, you're leaving?"

"Yeah." Toddle sat up, using the back of his hand to wipe his bleary, red-rimmed eyes. He laughed.

The word 'quitter' was on the tip of Wolfe's tongue, but he kept it down out of shame of even calling his friend that. He put his hand on Toddle's shoulder. "I understand. Where you heading to, then? A different position?"

He shook his head. "Nah, getting out of the city. Too many memories, not all of them good, you know? There's an open position for sheriff in the country, and I found a nice little house with an acre of woods."

"Sounds nice, very relaxing. Probably doesn't smell like trash there, either."

"Probably not," he said.

"Well... give me a call when you're settled, if you ever want to shoot the shit."

Toddle put out his hand. Wolfe took it. "Will do."

He rubbed his forehead against the steering wheel. Toddle hadn't called. It had taken some adjustment to being on his own. He had declined Conti's suggestion of a new partner. Wolfe had wanted to work alone, less balls in the air and all that, but now it felt like all he did was work twenty-four seven.

When it wasn't SSK it was other cases, sightings, suicides, robberies, et cetera. When it wasn't those, he spent what little time he had on the two cases he named '*The Women Without Eyes.*' Wolfe was the only one putting time in on them. Hell, he seemed to be the only one who *knew* about them.

There hadn't been a new victim since Tamira Davis, but he still pored over the same notes, lab reports, the interview with the witness, Toddle's notes from the family. He stared at the composite as if it would give him answers. The only new evidence was the cement particles found on Tamira's clothing, and that was hardly beneficial. The killer worked with or near cement, or just so happened to walk through some the day he killed Tamira. Much help that was.

The suspect's sketch did little to help, either. Despite being in circulation since March, he had never received a single phone call about a potential sighting, or someone who knew someone who looked similar. Wolfe figured most of the flyers were now in the city dump.

Wolfe felt overwhelmingly guilty. He still wasn't doing enough.

He'd been meaning to visit the library to research the symbol branded on the victims but either he never found the time, or it slipped his mind. His precious, little hours outside work were meant for Cindy and Tabby. He debated arranging a visit under the guise of a family trip, but it would end with him trying to be alone to work and inevitably failing because it was meant to be a family trip.

His phone buzzed in his pocket.

Cindy.

"Hey."

"Hi, sorry to call you, you must be at work now."

Wolfe looked through the windshield at the square gray building. Officers milled in and out of the front door. Some stood around by the cement stairs smoking. He set his head back down. "Just pulled in. What's up?"

"I was wondering if you could get next Saturday off for my parents' anniversary."

A groan began in his throat, and he held it there. He loved his wife more than anything, but he doubted Conti would let him off with Toddle gone. It was possible he'd be pulled to work the tip lines, non-stop ringing phones night and day.

"I can ask, but I doubt I'll get it."

"Why?"

He frowned. "What do you mean, 'Why?'"

"You don't ask for time off, and you work fifty, sixty hours a week. It's my parents, for God's sake."

"You know how it works. It's not like I'm working at a grocery store. If I'm not here, that's one less detective investigating a murder, one less pair of eyes that could lead to a breakthrough, and with Toddle gone, they need all the help they can get.

"Plus," he continued without thinking, regretting it as soon as he started, "he gave me the whole weekend off for Tabby's birthday."

She exhaled through clenched teeth. "You still worked the day of her party."

"I was home for it."

"You still worked on her birthday, Gary. It still felt like you stole the whole day from her." Silence, then: "Don't you ever get tired of working? Don't you miss us? It's always work first, family second."

"You're making it sound like I'm choosing this."

"Maybe that's the truth, and you're just lying to me and yourself. Maybe you prefer it."

"What the fuck are you talking about? I said I'd ask but told you what would probably happen. People are *dying*, haven't you seen the news? I don't get to pick and choose which days some asshole beats his wife, or when some depraved fuck gets jealous of his girlfriend. It's not like your job someone can cover your shift if you're sick. I have to be here for when it all goes down. Or don't you understand that?"

Inside the car was hot. Wolfe couldn't breathe.

"It's obvious you fucking love it more than us." Her voice rattled. Wolfe imagined tears. "I was dumb enough to believe that maybe when we had Tabby, she would make us your top priority, but apparently not." Cindy sniffled, sighed. "We never will be."

"Cindy..."

"Don't bother coming home tonight, Gary."

The line died in his hands.

He gritted his teeth and held back a building scream as the hard plastic dug into his palm. Then he launched the phone across the car, smacking the windshield, bouncing off the dashboard, and falling onto the passenger side floor.

Doesn't she fucking understand what I'm doing?

Doesn't she know I'm why killers are put away?

He lurched out of the car.

Calm down. Wolfe gathered himself together. *Push it down. Hold it there. You have work to do. Cases to solve. People are counting on you. Deal with Cindy later.*

Wolfe weaved around the boys in blue coming in and out of the station and made his way to his desk silently. Piles of paperwork greeted him. He didn't care about who or what it was, he just took a file from the top and started.

No one spoke to him the entire day. When Conti made his rounds around the precinct, he ignored Wolfe, too. When his shift ended, the detective went out and bought a coffee and a bag of pretzels, then returned to his desk. Opening the bottom cabinet, he pulled out a well-worn folder with '*The Women Without Eyes*' scribbled on the top.

William Acerieas

WILLIAM PARKED BEHIND THE museum. He looked out his windshield at the massive tan brick building, ablaze with dying sunlight, the pinking sky darkening above him. The last time he visited the museum was with his father before he'd been given over to the machine. That was ten years ago. He settled back into the seat with a sigh. He put his cell phone on his lap, crossed his arms, and closed his eyes.

They left the museum in the evening. The sky was cloudy, the horizon burning. William ran ahead carrying a plastic tyrannosaurus rex. Its jaws snapped when you pulled a string at the bottom of the handle. He made it chomp, giggling.

"Okay, okay," his father said, "calm down."

William shoved the toy in his father's face and made it snap again.

"All right, dino-boy." He pushed the toy aside and hunched to eye level. "Look, Will. Tomorrow..." He glanced away, then faced him again. "Tomorrow I'll be doing the Family Work and..." Tears lined his brown eyes. "I don't know if I'll see you again."

William didn't understand why his father was crying, why his hands trembled. He put his hand to his father's cheek, feeling the rough stubble pricking his skin. "It'll be okay, daddy. Pap-pap will keep you safe."

His father took his son's hand. "That's true. He will."

Then, his father's arms were wrapped around him and his body racked with soft sobs.

His ringing phone snapped him awake.

"Hello? William? It's Cindy. I'm running a little late, I just got my daughter home from her grandparents, and she spilled juice on the carpet and I couldn't let it stain. I'm on my way now. Should be another twenty minutes."

He coughed. His mouth was dry. He licked his lips and swallowed. "It's fine, no need to rush," he said as he stared at the purple sky through a veil of tears. He realized he was crying and cleared his eyes with his sleeve. Shadows collected in the alley between the museum and an abandoned red-brick building. Streetlamps automatically turned on. "Just call me when you're here."

"I will, I will, thank you." She hung up.

He set the phone on the dash and reached over the console for his duffel bag. He rechecked his gear. A chill covered his hands and face. Suddenly he wanted a scalding shower. Everything was there: hunting knife, blow torch and igniter, the Family Brand, plastic gloves, scalpel, grapefruit spoon and mason jar.

He pulled on the gloves and reclined, closing his eyes, trying to calm his anxiety. It felt only like five minutes passed when the phone rang again, but the dashboard clock told him thirty minutes had gone by. It was now fully dark.

"I'm here," Cindy said over the phone, "I found a spot out front."

"I parked in the back and the horse is a little heavy. Will you be able to park near me?"

She grumbled.

"I'll take off ten dollars, if that helps."

She didn't reply for a couple of seconds. "That's fine. I'll call you back."

Two minutes later, her maroon Sedan pulled in with its headlights on and parked a few spaces back. William took the knife and slid it up his left sleeve, then opened the door and got out. Clouds passed overhead and smothered the moonlight.

"Cindy?" he said.

"Hi, hello." She left her car running as she approached. She wore a yellow t-shirt under a denim jacket. A brown purse was slung over her shoulder. Her ink-colored hair melted into the night. "Sorry for being late, didn't think it would get this dark."

"Not a problem." He opened the trunk. The internal light ticked on, blanketing the rocking horse in a yellow glow. His extra clothes were in a trash bag behind it. She leaned forward with him as he pushed the horse's snout down and let it go. "See, it's quite old and it needs some new paint, but still works fine."

"I see." She glanced at her daughter sitting in the back of the Sedan. The child had a set of colorful keys in her hands. "She'll love it." She unzipped her bag and rummaged through it. "How much was it now, with the discount? Sixty-five?"

"That sounds about right." He bent his wrist to let the knife glide into his grasp. He scanned the lot again. No one was about, no cars but theirs. Cindy, holding a leather wallet, looked up. Her eyes widened. For a moment their gazes met, then she focused on the knife.

Time slowed for William. Tears grew and welled and fell, her lips opened, a scream surging up her throat but not making it to her mouth in time as he wrapped his arm around her head, spinning her around, holding her back to his body, and plunging the knife into the right side of her neck and wrenching it across. Gurgling blood halted her scream, spilling from her lips, gushing in rivulets from her throat. It pooled beneath her feet and soaked into William's sleeves and pant legs, as her body convulsed. He held her until she was quiet. He released her, and she dropped to the pavement.

Adrenaline flooded his system. He felt hot, no longer in a parking lot but in a lake of hellfire. His chest swelled with embers. His every breath smoldered, steam shooting from nose and mouth. The knife was heavy, *powerful*. He checked around him and when he saw no one, he beelined to the Sedan.

Children were undoubtedly pure innocence, an agreement in all walks of life. They knew nothing of violence, of good or bad, greed or gluttony. They *saw* the world in a way everyone else couldn't, and with that alone, they would make an Offering that much stronger.

His hand was on the door handle, the other still firmly holding the blade. The child giggled in her car seat, and dropped her toy keys. She tried to reach for them, but the belt wouldn't let her lean far enough. She began to cry. Her yellow-and-white striped shirt, jeans, and tiny shoes matched her mother's.

The flames inside William dwindled, dampening. The ground was no longer hellfire but cracked tarmac. His knife was light and weak. His breath was only air, not smoke. He felt small. Frail. Pathetic. His grip nearly loosened from the door, but he forced it open.

For the Family.

He retrieved the keys from the floor and handed them to the young girl. She took them in her chubby hand, jingled them, giggling.

For grandfather.

William placed his palm to her forehead. He gnawed on his lip to keep his cry in his throat.

For mother. For father.

He didn't look away. If he did, he'd never look back. Numb fingers fumbled with her buckles. With shaking arms, he picked her up to set her onto the ground.

For everyone.

After positioning the bodies, he sprinted to his car and threw everything in the duffel, now two mason jars heavier. Swiftly he changed into his clean clothes. He floored it out from the lot. There had been no interruptions like before; no witnesses, no mistakes. Vomit threatened to come but he forced it to stay in his gut. He was lucky the police weren't patrolling this district, to wrapped up in dealing with the SKK.

William felt like something outside of reality was helping him, ensuring his purpose was fulfilled. He liked to think it was his parents. He ran some red lights and stop signs, keeping the needle over 55 MPH. When the house came into view, he swung into the alley, narrowly missing the trash cans set out for the morning. The instant the car was in park he shoved open the door, fell onto the gravel, and retched.

He attempted to sit up but the strength in his arms had left him. William rolled onto his side and curled into the fetal position. Tears and snot mixed with the strings of saliva and sickness dribbling from the side of his mouth. The cool night air made no impression on the overwhelming heat radiating from him.

I had to do it.

It had to be done.

Blood and flayed flesh and eyes...

He puked again, his chest and gut aflame. Closing his eyes didn't help. The child, the mother, Mrs. Davis and the college student all danced across the back of his eyelids. They spun around him as though he lay in the center of a horrific merry-go-around. Over and over again their eyeless faces loomed over him, blood pouring from their gaping sockets.

Stop!

Please!

I had to!

It had to be done!

When he opened his eyes the world spun, then slowed, then stilled. The nightmare raged inside his head, but he willed his body to stand, willed his mind to focus on his one and only task.

I have to finish.

He reached into the car and grabbed the duffle from the seat. Walking to the house was like traversing waist-deep mud, every step making his stomach roll.

I'm at the end. Stopping now would make everything for nothing.

He almost fell down the cellar steps. He grabbed the rail and clung onto it. He removed the jars from the bag and tossed it into the side room. On his knees he set the jars onto the chair's seat. He ran his palms along the armrests, then balled his hands into fists and pounded the weathered wood over and over again. Fresh tears came.

Will these be enough?

Will I need more?

If so, can I continue?

Am I strong enough?

Barely keeping myself together now.

The damp air kept the vomit down. He raised his face to the vats, towering above him like gods.

It must be enough.

It has to be.

I cannot stop. I'm the only one left.

"Father. Mother. Grandfather." He said between sobs. "We'll be together soon."

May 12, 1994

Detective Wolfe

WOLFE HEARD A THUDDING somewhere far off. He ignored it and tried to focus on the warmth, the comfortability of sleep, but the thudding continued until it became so loud it filled his head like a gong.

A police officer stood outside the fogged passenger side window, tapping on the glass with the end of his flashlight.

Wolfe groaned, raising his seat, and rolled down the window. "Yeah?" A rancid taste coated his tongue, grit from alcohol and fast food on his teeth. Pungent body odor radiated from his greasy skin and unwashed clothes, and he hoped the officer couldn't smell him.

"You can't park here, sir." The officer peered into the car, trying to find something incriminating inside. The half-empty bottle of rum was tucked under the seat. The overcast sky was a sheet of gray.

"All right..." Wolfe read the officer's nameplate. "Sorry about that, *Anthony*, I'll move in a second."

"Better do it now, sir, or I'll be forced to give you a ticket."

Wolfe winced from a throbbing head. He stretched his neck and waved the officer away. "Yeah, yeah, I'm going. Can you move so I can get behind the wheel?"

The man stepped back.

"Thanks," Wolfe spat, getting out, walking around the front, and got into the driver's seat. The officer began to speak again, but Wolfe stabbed the keys into the ignition, started the engine, and drove away. The dashboard clock read: 11:48 AM.

Shit.

Should I try to go back home before work? Would Cindy let me in? Would she do it for Tabby?

He reached under his seat and found his phone beneath a paper bag.

No calls or messages. A few voicemails from Conti but he ignored those.

He shoved the phone in his pocket.

Let's see if she'll let me grab a shower, or at least let me brush my teeth.

The lights were off when he pulled into the driveway. Cindy's car was gone. A small bubble of uncertainty rose in the back of his mind, but Wolfe pushed it down. *It's Cindy's day off, so they're probably at her parents'.* He stupidly expected his key not to work, as if she had changed the locks overnight.

"Hello? Anyone home?"

Silence.

Wolfe checked the kitchen, the dining room, went into the living room. "Cind? Tabby?"

Uncertainty turned to fear.

He took the stairs two at a time. Both Tabby's room and the bathroom in the hall were empty. In their bedroom, he phoned Cindy, who didn't pick up. His fingers shook as he went through his contacts and failed to find her parents' number.

Shit!

He called his parents instead and got the answering machine.

"Hey, it's Gary. Just wondering if you've heard from Cindy. I think she's at her parents', probably still sleeping, but I wanted to check up. Call me back if you hear anything. Thanks."

Like you said, she's probably sleeping or forgot to charge her phone. Everything's fine. No reason to panic or worry. They're at her parents to get away from the house, to get away from you.

He turned the shower on and, while the water warmed, checked his phone, again, to find no new calls or messages.

I'll call again after I'm done.

He called after he got dressed. And again, in his car, again driving to work.

No answer. No answer. No answer.

By the time he parked, the fear was all-consuming, weighing on his shoulders. His stomach burned.

He tried to remember Cindy's parents' number once more, but could only recall the area code.

I'll get it from someone inside.

People eyed him as he walked to his desk. Some kept their faces to their work, the wall, the framed photos of previous generations of law enforcement.

I wasn't that much of an asshole yesterday, was I?

The Captain's door swung open when he stepped into the bullpen. "Wolfe?"

"Yeah?"

"Get in here."

"Why? What happened?"

"Just get your ass in here."

Wolfe looked around Everyone kept their eyes away.

What the hell is going on?

"Shut the door and sit down," Conti said when he entered.

He did.

Conti's face was blotchy red, and it looked like he hadn't slept in a few days. A cigarette burned between his fingers, and an empty glass sat by the full ashtray on his desk. There was a bottle of rye near a pile of papers. His hand shook when he took a drag, and he sighed out exhaust and flicked ash into the heap.

"Look, Wolfe, Gary," he started. "I don't know how to say this..."

He knew the words before they left Conti's lips. The signs that morning was so apparent now that he found it hard to believe he had been so stupid to mistake them as him being overbearing. Fear became terror. Horror. His stomach dropped into his pelvis and the only thing holding his insides together was fraying sinew.

"We received a call about two bodies, a mother and a child, behind the Cherry Brooke Museum…"

The world titled. Conti's desk wavered. Darkness encroached his vision, seeping through the corners of the room.

"…I sent a few of our own out, Wilkinson…"

Wolfe gripped the armrests with numb hands, his rubbery fingers unable to find purchase on the faded wood. Shadows danced from the floor, swaying along the walls in a topsy-turvy hell. Lead replaced his bones and Wolfe fought to keep his head raised and remain conscious.

"…when they called, I went out myself to make sure they were right…"

Everything crashed over him and he took the chair with him.

Sheets of black covered the walls and he thought he screamed. He might never have stopped. The nothingness above dropped over him and when it devoured him, he cursed it for not coming sooner.

Hours, days, later, he wasn't certain, Wolfe came to on the couch. The window overlooking the front yard was dark. A sodium lamp burned orange in the night. Shadows filled the house. The kitchen light was on, falling into the living room. On the coffee table was a note written in chicken scratch.

Gary

You passed out in my office but I figured you wouldn't want to deal with an ambulance or the hospital so I got you home. You looked fine besides passing out but I'm no doctor. You just need sleep. You were still out when I left mumbling something.

Anyway, I'm sorry about everything. We're pulling all our resources to find the fucker who did this. Don't worry about having to ID them, her parents are coming down to do it.

The bastard will rot in a cell I promise.

Take as much time off as you need and let me know if you want more after that.

Conti

P.S. I put a unit on your street. With the way things are and your gun in my desk (couldn't let you keep it during this sort of thing you understand), he'll only be around a few times a day. It's not much I know, but it's better than nothing.

Wolfe let the letter fall as he sank back into the sofa. He wet his dry lips and tasted the tang from sleeping with his mouth open.

The dissociative feeling of not being himself remained, as if he was watching another person move his body. When he clenched his hands, they felt wrong, fake, as if someone had created a replica of himself. He looked around the room. He wasn't meant to be here without them, it was like desecrating the sanctuary they once built, shared. Wolfe planted someone else's feet onto the floor.

He wanted out.

Out of the house.

Out of his life.

Out of anything not involving Cindy and Tabby.

What was the point staying around without them?

What sort of monstrosity would he be to keep living in the house they bought together? Lived in together. Laughed, danced, fought, cried, made love in. It was more than the house; it was their shared existence, bad or good.

What does one do when their reason for living was gone?

He slouched forward, stood, stumbled, found his balance, trudged into the kitchen. In the highest cabinet above the counter, past the Tupperware, he took down the bottle of rum they kept for special occasions. *Like the night she bought me that watch.*

Nothing worthwhile on the horizon anymore, so he spun off the cap, clattering to the floor. He took a long pull, stopped, breathed, took another. Wolfe drank until the bottle was as empty as he felt and chucked the bottle at the sink. It exploded, shattered glass splashing the counter.

His phone vibrated in his pocket. Conti must've slipped it in there. The world smeared and he couldn't make out the text on the small screen at first, but he focused and, with difficulty, read the date in the upper-right hand corner.

May 12, 1994.

Cindy. Tabby.

Notes, dates, reports, files, all barreled through his mind.

Susan Tanaka.

January 11, 1994.

Tamira Davis.

March 11, 1994.

A single image eclipsed all the others. He became present. In the moment. His body was now his own. His eyes widened and he opened his mouth to speak but didn't know what to say. All warmth drained from him and he felt like wax, melting and pooling over the floor.

Cindy.

Tabitha.

May 11, 1994.

He tried to break his fall, but his hands slipped on the kitchen table and he collided with the hardwood, cracking his head.

"I told him." He slurred like a giant baby or drunk man. "Told... him..."

He embraced the impending sleep.

MAY 13, 1994

Gary Wolfe

"GARY. GARY, WAKE UP."

Wolfe mumbled and pushed away the hand on his shoulder.

"Gary, wake up. You're on the damn floor."

The void ebbed, bloomed into dull yellows and greens, and slowly filled with sunlight coming through the backdoor window.

He coughed into the floor and slowly rolled onto his back.

Conti stood over him, his hands in his pockets.

"Morning."

"How'd you get in?"

"I took your keys last night. Wanted to make sure you didn't think of driving or going anywhere."

Wolfe coughed again and wiped his mouth on his arm. He sat up and the room rotated. When it settled, he stood and slumped into one of the kitchen chairs. He put his face into his hands, moaning.

"Do you want anything? Coffee? Food?"

"A gun would be nice."

"Don't say that shit, Gary."

The memories from the previous night rose from the rippling pool of his mind. He remembered before he fell. Dates. Susan. Tamira. His family. It was the same person, the one who took the eyes every other month and branded them. The coincidences couldn't be ignored.

Wolfe peered through his fingers. Conti brushed the broken glass on the counter into the sink with a rag, and grabbed the carafe.

"I hate to do this, Gary," he said, filling the coffee pot, and shoving the carafe into the machine. "Especially now. But you know how this goes." He closed the lid and switched it on. Percolating filled the room. "Where were you on the night of May 10th?"

He raised his palms in advance of Gary's tirade. "I don't believe for a second you did it, but wives and husbands are killed, and we look at their spouses. I have to ask."

Wolfe pushed himself onto his feet. He swayed for a moment, steadied. "I worked late. Worked on the case that you refused to listen to me about. Then I slept in my damn car. Cindy and I had an argument about Tabby's birthday that morning. I parked in front of some restaurant, and a uni woke me up the next morning, Anthony Pulz, or something, it was Italian. You can check."

"You never drove anywhere or left?"

"Christ." It was like being smacked across the face. Now he knew how people felt when he asked the same questions. He hoped he'd never have to ask it again. "Just get the hell out of my house. This is your fault, anyway."

"My fault?"

"Yeah, your fault. You didn't listen to me. Not enough resources because it was a kid and a grandmother. If you would've fucking listened, this wouldn't have happened. They'd still be here."

The Captain walked past Wolfe to the hallway. "C'mon, you can't be serious."

"Get the fuck out!" He screamed into Conti's face. Hot rage surged through his veins. "You let this happen! I told you he had done this before and would do it again, but you just fucking let him go, you let him go because he wasn't murdering important people, *white* people, and now look what he's done!"

Conti stepped onto the porch and Wolfe slammed the door in his face. He locked it and stomped back into the kitchen as a car started and peeled out on the street.

He sat into the chair and stewed. The only sound in the house was the coffee pot hissing. After what might have been either two hours or two days, he went upstairs. He stood in front of their bedroom, letting memories play: the gray eggshell paint Cindy insisted on using when they moved in, the matching rosewood nightstands they picked out together, the hand-embroidered pillows they received as wedding gifts sitting on top the black comforter they made love in, where Tabby became more than just an idea, where they fought, slept, their entire marriage boiling down to one small room where days always began and ended, no matter how upset with each other they were or were not.

He went to Tabby's room. He looked over the pictures tacked to the pink walls, her floral bedspread, the toys and stuffed animals scattered across the white carpet. In the corner was the hamper for all her old clothes and toys, one that would've grown with time. In the other corner, a small bookshelf half-full of handed down books Cindy and he had gotten when they were kids themselves.

Both places appeared the same, as though only waiting for his family's return, yet the colors were washed out, lifeless and dull. They never would return, rooms forever husks of the beautiful lives they once contained... He went into the hallway bathroom, turned the shower on, sat on the toilet, and cried.

Wolfe left the shower when the hot water had turned too cold to bear. After toweling off, he put on sweats and an old t-shirt and went back downstairs. He didn't know where to go or what to do. No longer was there a path to follow, an anchor keeping him where he was meant to be. He drifted from the living room to the kitchen to the entryway, back to the kitchen, to the living room.

He ignored the calls from his parents, from Cindy's parents, from anyone trying to reach him. People knocked on the door throughout the day but he ignored those, too. He didn't want to talk, to release the swirling loss. Pain coalesced inside him.

Memories burned in his mind like the seared brands he'd looked at over and over again.

He saw Cindy's face, her blue eyes, the dates they went on. Movies. Diners. Driving aimlessly on the back roads outside of the city until the early hours of the morning, enraptured by one another, the only two people in the world. Their wedding day, the way her hair was done up beautifully, how her gown fit perfectly to her body, how her red lips smiled as she said "I do", their first kiss as husband and wife.

The first time held Tabby in their hospital room, how small and dainty she was, beautiful as her mother, how she had his soft brown hair and her mother's eyes, her first birthday and the cake she smeared across the baby seat, running it through her hair and letting clumps plop to the ground, her last birthday party, taking her to the park with his parents, the museum with Cindy's family, taking her out into her grandparents' long stretch of yard that ended with a line of giant evergreens and Tabby staring up at them in awe as if she were peering up at gods...

More and more flashbacks rolled through his mind. More and more waxed and waned until his temples throbbed. In every room he went through he broke down, unable to stop the flood that had to run its course. He avoided the bedrooms. Wolfe lingered in their door but never went in. His intrusion would solidify that his family was truly gone, never to return.

Night came and he was on the couch. Two empty bottles of wine they had received for an anniversary present lay at his feet. He held a third bottle. His head lolled, his mouth stained purple, grape coating his tongue, cloying his throat. The living room's patterned wallpaper rippled, a wavering watercolor painting.

Something fell and crashed. He blinked. His head rested on the cushion. His feet were wet and sticky. A black circle closed in on his vision until nothing remained but an absolute darkness he prayed would never leave.

May 15, 1994

Gary Wolfe

"Jesus," someone said.

Wolfe's bleary eyes rolled in their sockets. A shadowy figure stood in the doorway. He rubbed his eyes on the couch cushion that stunk of sweat and wine. The silhouette filled with features: brown eyes, small nose, a brown hat, and a tan jacket.

"Toddle?"

"Who else?" Toddle made his way through the pizza boxes and beer cans that were on the floor.

Wolfe sat up. "What're you doing here?"

"Conti called. I heard what happened. I'm so sorry."

Wolfe waved his hand. "Not your fault. It's Conti's."

"He mentioned something about that. You think it's the guy who did those other two?"

"I know it is."

Toddle shook his head. "How're you holding up, besides the obvious?"

Wolfe gestured at the room. "How do you think?"

"Yeah, I could smell this place from outside. How'd you manage to get all this booze with the uni outside?"

Wolfe laughed. "Delivery when the cruiser's gone, someone will always deliver for enough money."

"Any left for me?"

"I'm sure there's something down there that hasn't been opened." He groaned as he sat forward, groped through the empties at his feet until he found an unopened can still on the plastic ring. "Probably warm. Don't remember when I got it. Or what day it is."

"It's the 15ᵗʰ, and thanks." Toddle cracked it open and sipped the rising foam.

"15ᵗʰ... Four days."

Not in front of Toddle.

"So," Toddle said, "what's your plan now?"

"Plan?"

"Yes, plan. You know who did this, so how're you going to go after him?"

Wolfe shrugged.

"I'd call Martin—he's still the head ME, right?—and get those reports. You've probably been avoiding the details, and I don't blame you. I wouldn't want to see my family like that either. But the only way to nail this asshole is to do your job. Then, with a favor or two," he continued, smirking, "have someone grab your shit from your desk and bring them here. After that it's just good old fashioned detective work."

"What if I don't want to do it the legal way?"

Toddle sighed, took a swig from the can, and set it on the coffee table. "I can't tell you what to do, only that you try. If you catch my drift."

He slapped Wolfe's knee and stood. "Anyway, I gotta' go. Sorry I can't stay any longer. I don't have any time off yet, and it's a bit of a drive into the city, but I'll give you a call soon. We can hit up a bar or something." He glanced at the debris at his feet. "If you don't open up your own beforehand."

Wolfe looked down at his lap. "Yeah, we'll do that soon. Thanks for coming by."

"Don't mention it. I'll see you, and again, I'm so sorry."

Toddle moved through the litter and left. Wolfe listened to his car door shut, the engine kick on, and his former partner fade into the distance.

He found his cell phone barely charged under the sofa. It smelled of beer and its buttons were sticky. He scrolled past the voicemails to the lab's number and dialed.

"Hello?" a man said on the other end.

"Put Martin on."

"Who is this?"

"Just tell him it's Gary."

The sound of muffling on the other side.

"Wolfe?"

"Yes."

"Hey, how's it going? I'm so sorry..."

"Is there any way you can get me their labs?"

"Who?" he said, dumbly.

"You know who."

"I, uh, why?"

"Doesn't matter. Can you get them to me or not?"

"I, yeah, I can. To your house?"

"Please. Thanks Martin."

Wolfe hung up, then searched his contacts for someone who wouldn't mind doing him a favor, and was surprised he had Detective Wilkinson's number. He vaguely remembered he'd got it at one of the police dive bars some time ago. Although Wolfe barely knew him, he hoped he'd help him out.

"Hello?"

"Wilkinson? Wolfe."

"Hey Gary, what's going on? Sorry to hear about everything."

"Thanks. Listen, do you think you could do me a favor?"

"With what just happened? I'd do anything to help, Gary. Lost my wife to the Big C a year ago if you remember, around October, and it tore me apart. Didn't have any kids though, thank God."

"Wilkinson?"

"Sorry, what do you need?"

"There's a manila folder in the bottom right drawer in my desk. Says '*The Women Without Eyes*' on it. Can you get that to me?"

Wilkinson chuckled. "I'm off today. How soon do you want it?"

"If you can, by the end of day, or early tomorrow would be nice."

"You'll have it by five today, you have my word."

"Thanks Wilkinson." He fell silent, anxiety swelling inside him. "There's another thing I need."

"What is it?"

"The reports on my family."

"Gary..."

"I know it's a lot to ask, and breaking protocol, but I have to know."

"I can try to get a copy, but can't guarantee anything."

"Thank you. A lot. I mean it." He felt like he should offer something, maybe a beer or a chat about lost loves, but he had more important things on his mind. "I'll see you then, thanks again."

"No problem, buddy."

Wilkinson wore brown pants, a white shirt, and had two folders under his arm. When Wolfe let him in, he bear-hugged him before he could prepare for it, burying Wolfe's face into his soft chest.

"I know I've said it before, but I'm so sorry, Gary. When my wife passed, God, I was a wreck."

Wolfe gave a muffled reply.

Wilkinson released him and patted him on the shoulder. "It'll be okay. You'll get through this, trust me."

"I'm going to try," he said. "Did the uni outside hassle you?"

Wilkinson shook his head. "I know Ralf. Good guy. I used to work the same beat as him when I wore the blue."

"Are those the files?" Wolfe pointed.

"Oh, yes." Wilkinson handed them over. "All there. If anyone asks how you got them, don't say it was me." He laughed, then fell into an awkward silence. "Look, Gary, what's in that report isn't going to help. You know that, right? Knowing can sometimes hurt worse than not knowing."

"I know, I know, but, hey, look, I'm pretty tired and..."

"Say no more. I'll get out of your hair. Just remember what I said, okay?"

"I will. Thank you again."

Wilkinson hugged him once more and then took his leave. Wolfe scanned the quiet street and found the uni gone. He hoped Martin would arrive soon.

He set the unopened files on the kitchen table and waited.

An hour passed.

With nothing left to drink and not wanting to drown in the drink again, he decided to clean up. Beer cans, wine bottles, pizza boxes and takeout containers, all were swept into a garbage bag. He didn't recall eating chips but there were a few bags beneath the sofa, and crumbs on the blankets, pillows, and between the cushions. After tossing the trash and vacuuming the place, another hour had passed.

No Martin.

Fucking hell.

The throw rug was stained purple, and chips were caked into the fibers. Wolfe ripped it from the floor and tossed it out the back door along with another trash bag. He'd never liked it anyway. He scrubbed what stains he could out from the couch.

He threw the pillows in the wash, not knowing if they could be machine washed or not. Cindy had typically done most of the cleaning, he stuck to basics like vacuuming and wiping down things.

There was a knock at the front door. Wolfe halted. Another knock. He hurried to the door and peeked out the window.

Martin's glasses gleamed under the porch light. He still wore his baby blue scrubs and a wrinkled, white lab coat. He had a file in his hand and car keys in the other.

Wolfe opened the door.

"Here you go." He shoved the file into Wolfe's hands. "Took a while for everyone to leave, so I could make copies. Couldn't have people asking questions, you know?"

Wolfe opened the file, skimmed the pages. "Everything's here, right?"

"Every little speck." Martin glanced over his shoulder and Wolfe followed his stare. A woman sat in his car.

Wolfe wanted to ask if it was Andria, the assistant who forgot two separate things with the previous labs, but thought better of it. "Thanks again, Martin." He jutted his chin towards the car. "Enjoy yourself tonight. Be safe, too."

Martin laughed. "I'll try. Have a good night."

"You too."

He closed the door and when Martin got into his car, Wolfe killed the porch light.

Now that he had everything he wanted, Wolfe moved his thoughts to something far more important. He had forced himself not to think about it, had ignored phone calls from both his and Cindy's parents, and submerged himself into a drunken oblivion. But he had come out the other end. The want to disappear was replaced by the drive to put the man who stole everything from him in the ground.

Wolfe needed to schedule what his family deserved as soon as possible. He'd put it off for far too long. He opened the phone book and searched '*F*' for what he required.

Merritt & Son Funeral Services.

Unexpectedly, even at this time of night, they picked up on the first ring.

May 17, 1994

Gary Wolfe

THE GRAY SKIES DISSIPATED as they stood in the dewy grass of the graveyard. Streaks of sunlight passed over the two sealed coffins. Everyone wore black. Cindy's parents stood on one side of the caskets, Wolfe and his parents on the other. Behind them were cousins and uncles and aunts Wolfe only spoke to during the holidays. His father's hand rested on his shoulder. Toddle stood nearby with dozens of others from the precinct. Conti wasn't there. Cindy's friends, bleary eyed, were at the rear, along with the couples from the neighborhood whose children were friends with Tabby.

After Cindy's parents and one of her friends spoke, the preacher stepped forward. Wolfe couldn't focus on anything except the caskets, and the priests' words didn't make it to him. He fought back tears. Even with the cool morning air, he was hot, his clothes suffocating him.

"And, so," the preacher's continued, "these beautiful souls make their way into Heaven and join God's children in their peaceful, blissful life there. Amen."

Everyone muttered, "Amen."

"Now, Gary would like to say a few words before the lowering of the caskets." The preacher retreated.

Wolfe sighed. It was like walking uphill to the front of the gathering. "I wasn't the best husband or father in the world." His voice sounded wrong, a croaky, weak timbre in place of his own. "But I made sure they never wanted for anything. I spent too much time away. Too busy working on what I thought was important. Now I'm realizing what was most important was at home." Wolfe touched Cindy's casket. "If I could go back, I would in a heartbeat." He let out a stifled laugh. "Maybe I wouldn't have been in law enforcement. Maybe I should've worked somewhere else."

He stopped.

"Sorry, I'm rambling. I just wish that I could take everything back and restart with them. I wish I could be home more, be there on the weekends, make sure what was happening in my life was happening in their lives as well, but I can't." *But what I can do is make sure the bastard who did this won't do it again.*

"I love you and miss you, more than you could ever know," he said to them, returning to his spot by Toddle, who nodded to him.

Two thickset men in navy blue work-suits walked to the graves. They attached a wire to the device beneath the coffins.

"Now, we lower the caskets," said the preacher.

The men pressed a trigger at the end of the wires, and the caskets slowly lowered. When they came to rest, they removed the golden bars outlining the graves and pulled out the lowering straps.

One by one, each attendee walked by them and said their goodbyes. Some tossed roses onto the caskets, others simply stared in silence, then everyone gradually left. Wolfe watched them go until he was the last one there. He didn't go near the holes, but stood back and stared down into them. It was the last time he would be close to them, the last time they would be together as a family. He knew once he got into his car, he would no longer be a father or a husband. He'd just be Gary Wolfe.

It wasn't until late in the afternoon that the workers returned with shovels and wheelbarrows. They didn't say he had to leave, but he took the hint. They told him he could come back after they were done, or just move away while they worked. Wolfe wanted it all to end but felt compelled to stay, as if the more time he was there, the closer to redemption he was, the more chance they'd forgive him from Heaven. He walked away, halted, turned, walked, stopped, turned, over and over again until he made it to his car.

He got in and watched the men shovel dirt until both were filled. After they left, and long after it was too difficult to see in the dark, Wolfe started his car and drove home.

MAY 18, 1994

William Acerieas

HE HAD BEEN WRONG.

There wasn't enough.

The number of Offerings required wasn't written in the Book, and grandfather had never told him. He'd always said he 'eyeballed it.' Even now, William wasn't sure if he'd been joking or serious. To him, the sparse layer of Offerings at the bottom of the vats wasn't adequate and he didn't want to chance using the machine and waste it.

He paced the Family Crest carved into the floor, looking over the chair, the vats, the tubing. His eyes burned, and he couldn't remember the last time he slept through the night. He scratched his forehead and felt oily dirt under his fingernails. He didn't dare to touch his hair, already knowing what would come back. With every waft from under his shirt, the stench of his body stung his nose.

I can't harvest more. It's not in me anymore.

He told me they were only things to power the machine, to further the Family's task. But...

They were people. Living, breathing people. William couldn't break them down into his sole purpose anymore, no matter how hard he tried. His Family was the most important thing in the world to him, but he couldn't bring himself to go out and get more. *I might be caught being like this. I'll make a mistake that'll leave me in handcuffs. They'll give* me *the chair.*

He stopped before the machine.

"I wish you were still here, so I didn't have to do this alone."

His father flashed through his mind, his brown hair, eyes, the way he had looked like William looked now. He had taught him how to have fun alongside his studies, how to build snowmen in the winter, jump in leaves in the fall. He'd taught him to use a tarp and water to slide across the lawn in the summer. His father had been nothing like his grandfather, a son only by blood. He'd been warm and understanding, willing to do what he could for William, taking the brunt of grandfather's verbal lashing when William didn't live up to his expectations.

There's still one option left.

Turning away, he took the ladder leaning against the wall and propped it in front of a vat. He took the key from beneath the workbench and removed the padlock from the closet under the clock. The hinges on the closet squeaked and he looked over the shelf of yellowed jars. Offerings older than he was looked back.

Alone, they would be practically useless, but together with the ones left by grandfather and the fresh ones he had obtained, they could be enough. Each was differently colored and shaped—children, adults, infants, elders—some degraded and opaque with white film, while some could still be seen within the misty formaldehyde.

Taking one at random, he went and climbed the ladder, and unscrewed the lid. A vile aroma blew into his face as he upturned it. On the way down to get another jar, he carelessly chucked the glass against the wall, where it exploded.

Another flash of memory. His mother, his beautiful mother. Her brown hair and eyes that matched his own. Where grandfather had been unforgiving and brutal, she was kind and welcoming. Always there for him when he cried, when he fell, when he needed someone to confide in. She taught him that although they were different from other families, he was still normal, nothing less than anyone else. He couldn't admit it then but when William lost her it felt like losing more of himself than it had done with his father.

He returned to the closet and grabbed another, returned to the ladder, dumped it, smashed the jar.

His grandfather was all he had after them; all he knew. He loved him in his own way, but he'd been ruthless, drilling the Book into his skull until he could recite passages verbatim. There was no time for mistakes. He *must* carry on the tradition; he *must* finish their work. Didn't he love his grandfather? Didn't he want to be with his parents again? Did he want to be a failure not only to himself but his entire family? Sleepless nights, eye-bleeding mornings, endless days spent hunched over books and training with a knife and scalpel, the brand, learning the intricacies of the vats and machine as the world went on outside the house and—

Why did you make us do this?

Jar. Vat. Smash. Again.

"I wish they didn't leave."

Again.

"I wish they stayed."

Again.

"I wish they had told grandfather no."

Another. Another. Dump, throw, dump, throw.

"I wish the Family hadn't forced anyone."

Gleaming shards littered the floor.

"I wish everything could restart and they could be back and alive and we would've stopped all this from the beginning."

William fell to his knees. The cellar spun around him and he pushed his dirty palms into his eyes and sobbed.

"But I can't stop," he said to himself. "Too far along and I can't abandon everything they sacrificed themselves for." He hacked and coughed. *What else would I do? Where would I go? This is all I know. There are no other options left.* He got his feet under him. "Have to finish this. For them."

May 19, 1994 — May 20, 1994

Gary Wolfe

Night shifted to dawn, soft twilight filtering through the kitchen window. Wolfe sat hunched over the table, covered with photographs, reports, witness statements, a suspect composite, and anything else he could possibly get his hands on. His family's file remained closed.

Have to pull the Band-Aid off at some point.

He rubbed his stinging eyes, and quickly flipped open the manila cover.

Three black-and-white Polaroids were paperclipped to the top. Cement filled his gut.

First photo. The cement became a glacier.

Cindy sat against a brick wall, Tabby between her mother's crossed legs. Cindy's left hand rested on her daughter's head, and her other was held against Tabby's stomach. His daughter's hands were cupped on her mother's right hand, her small head bent forward.

Second photo. The iceberg exploded.

A close-up of the brand, the same as on the other women, on the nape of Cindy's neck, just beneath her splayed hair.

Third photo. The chunks melted, acidic bile rising up his esophagus.

Two close-ups of each face from below. Their sockets were empty, and slits ran across their throats. Blood soaked their clothes.

Wolfe sprinted to the kitchen sink, toppling the chair over, and lurched over the rim just in time. Minutes later, he returned to the table with a cup of water in hand. Wolfe wiped away the saliva and tried again. The police report gave no new information, except that the Museum's front security cameras caught Cindy driving past at 6:48 PM. A pixilated, low-resolution photo showed her car. The shops across the street were closed, and blurry figures milled around on the sidewalk.

He looked at the lab report.

No drugs or alcohol were found in either of their systems. The slashes went from right to left, like Tamira Davis. Adriana, the ME assistant, put their times of death at approximately 7:30 PM.

Wolfe flipped the page.

No DNA, fingerprints, semen or penetration. *Thank the fucking Lord.*

Nothing before him had answers to the questions burning in his mind. *Why were they there? Why did Cindy take Tabby out that late? Why didn't she call him? Why?*

He snatched the Polaroids from the other files and lined them up.

Susan, Tamira, Cindy and Tabby.

All had their eyes removed.

All had their throats cut.

All had been positioned in a ritualistic way, with their hands wrapped around their backs, street poles, splayed on the sidewalk, et cetera

All had the same brand.

Susan had been cut by someone right-handed, the others left-handed. He ignored that for now. The specifics didn't matter anymore. He chalked it up to the killer being ambidextrous, however uncommon it may be. There was no other explanation besides a copycat killer, but that was more impossible for him to believe. Presumably no one knew or cared enough about these murders to take up the killer's MO.

He wrote *ambidextrous* on a legal pad.

Another difference between Susan and the others was the drugs in her system. The ME suggested a sleep medication, something she took before the attack. It was possible she was drugged because she was the youngest of the bunch, and therefore riskier to manage; she could run, scream, et cetera.

How would he drug her before death? Did the killer know her? Meet her prior to the attack? It was injected, so it was possible it happened at the start of it. It makes sense it would be Susan, due to how clean everything was.

At the end of the day, it didn't matter who was or wasn't drugged, only that they were killed in the same way. Another question unanswered. Wolfe moved on.

Refleski Lake.

Cherry Brooke Public Library.

Cherry Brooke Museum.

All well-known, public places, but the times of death were different. Susan was at 3 AM, Tamira 1 AM, and his family 7:30 PM. The second murder seemed rushed, but that was most likely due to the witness. The third attack seemed *extra* rushed, changing the pattern by several hours. *Maybe the killer couldn't wait until after it was fully dark? Maybe he needed the job done ASAP? Maybe he saw his chance and just took it? Maybe he's gotten careless? Maybe the timing doesn't matter?*

He wrote: *Murders in evenings/night. Public places. Significance? If so, what? Places he knew? Accustomed to? Maybe childhood? Comfortability?*

Why take their eyes? Use them? Consume them?

He bit the end of his pen, then: *Positions also important, clearly. Doesn't come off as Satanic, but not normal. Religious? Likely. Occult? Even more likely.*

Roadblocks. He changed course, setting the photos aside and bringing over the photographs of the brandings.

The first branding was cleaner than the others, with no smudges or smears. He'd taken his time and ensured it came out exactly the way he seemingly wanted.

The second was sloppier. Not only because he was interrupted, but it was though he didn't know how much pressure to apply. The first was just on the skin, not deep enough to reveal the sinew beneath. With this one, although it was a black-and-white photo, shreds of muscle peeked out from the deep lines.

The third branding was cleaner than the second, but still not as good as the first. Still tiny tears showed muscle. He'd improved but probably only because he wasn't stopped in the act.

Wolfe drew a line from *ambidextrous* to *branding*. Then wrote across it: *Connection? Right-handed but used left for the last two kills? Why? Injured? Arthritis in the right? Just decided to change it up?*

The symbol had importance without a doubt, but it was lost on him. His mind turned back to religion. It would make sense with the way they were posed, but it didn't look like any religious symbol he ever saw, or any gang insignia he knew of. It was occult-like, an uglier pentagram.

A cult? He wrote. *Have I been an idiot this whole time and it's not one killer but a whole team of them? Everything screams the occult. Surprised I didn't see it until now. If it's a cult, how big is it? It would give the eye removal sense. They need them for something. Along with the poses, it's a safe bet it's for a ritual.* He crossed out his earlier notes about the eyes. *Do they have a leader? A god?*

He stared at his notes, tapping the pen on the pad, his brow furrowed.

Then, he turned to a new sheet, took the cleanest up-close Polaroid, and drew the symbol the best he could. He now had time to do the research he couldn't before. It was bittersweet. He shoved his things into his pocket and grabbed his keys on the way out.

In front of the Cherry Brooke Public Library, Wolfe glanced at the spot where they found Tamira. Framed photographs, flowers, dedications and other memorabilia lay by the lamp pole.

Tamira against the lamppost.

Blood down her neck.

Gash across her throat.

Clothes soaked in blood.

Eyes.

He headed inside.

An older woman in an olive-green turtleneck sat behind a polished oak counter. Wolfe recalled her from Tamira Davis's crime scene, the woman Wilkinson spoke to.

"Hello, can I help you?"

"I'm wondering if you have anything on old symbols?"

"What sort of symbols?"

He shrugged, laughing. "Old ones? Like ancient symbols. It'll just be easier to show you."

He placed his opened notepad onto the counter. She leaned forward, and a lock of graying hair slipped out from behind her ear.

"Huh," she said. "Never seen anything like it before... Maybe, try aisle S, column twelve, near the back corner to the right. Might have something you're looking for down there."

He thanked her. "Also, do you have that thing that has old newspaper articles?"

"A microfilm?"

"Yeah, that."

"Yes, it's in the back, and only for library members. If you want to use that, you'll need to register for a library card."

"Wonderful."

Past the empty tables, the seating area with two vacant couches facing each other, the racks of magazines, he entered the rows upon rows of books.

G.

K.

N.

Getting closer.

P.

R.

"S."

He scanned each column until he found column twelve. A label on the top shelf read: *Symbols, Sigils, & Other Religious Artifacts.*

There were only a dozen or so cellophane coated books, and Wolfe didn't know where to begin, so he grabbed them all in both arms and found a small table near the back. He sat and took the top one from the stack.

He set the fifth book aside with a sigh. Nothing so far matched his symbol. The next title read: *Family Trees & Crests.*

"Here we go."

He skimmed the glossy pages. There were some similar symbols, but either the lines were off or the outline was shaped differently. Nothing was a fit.

He stopped, and his grip on the book tightened.

Is that it?

He took his drawing and held it next to the picture on the page. Checked it again.

This was it.

It wasn't a cult symbol, but a family crest belonging to the Acerieas family. The book traced the family back to the 1600s, the pages filled with oval portraits of the oldest couple of the family: Jacob and Katherine Acerieas. Black lines branched down to their three children—Joanna, Cecily, John—and spread out to twelve more, three children apiece, then another set of family members. The family tree stopped short before the bottom margin, ending in 1937 with Johnathan and Donna Acerieas.

Wolfe flipped to the front of the book, checking the copyright page. The book was published in 1948.

He marked the page with a scrap of paper from his notes and rushed to the front desk.

"Do you have an updated version of this book, like a second edition or something?" He showed the cover.

The librarian frowned. "I don't know. Let me check." She turned to the small gray computer and typed. After a moment she shook her head. "No, nothing. If you'd like, I could get you the number of the publisher and see if they might be able to provide you with updated information. Or you can try the Microfilm reader, it won't be as thorough as the book, but there might be some newer articles for what you're looking for."

Better try the Microfilm first before getting the runaround by the publisher.

"I'd like to try the reader, thanks."

After signing up for a card he would never use, Wolfe was ushered into a small backroom. Stacks of papers lay atop filing cabinets shoved against the walls. The Microfilm reader sat in the back. He set *Family Trees & Crests* open on his lap with his notes on top.

He pressed his eyes into the cushioned viewfinder and rotated the wheel to the 1800s, the earliest it would go. He figured that if there was a pattern and the brands were connected to the family and the killings, then the murders wouldn't have been recent. They would've started a long time ago.

Scrolling ahead in time after reading each article, he searched for any reports with women found without eyes, or with any of the victims' traits. When he reached 1960, he sat back and rubbed a kink in his neck. Nothing concrete yet. Some reports matched some aspects, such as slit throats or being abandoned in public places, but the grainy black-and-white photos suggested that they weren't placed in a ritualistic pose or, from what he could tell, branded.

Maybe I'm going too fast.

Wolfe put his eyes to the viewfinder again and returned to the 1800s. In his gut, he felt he was close. The information was here, but he didn't know where to look. He had the name and the crest, he just needed something else.

Slowly, temples throbbing, he read through the articles again.

1805... 1810... 1815... 1820... 1825... 1827...

Here was something. Between 1827 and 1830, there was a string of murders reported throughout a small town off the eastern coast of Pennsylvania. The article only had a few sentences, but the victims had all been female (possibly working girls), their eyes removed using some sort of utensil (farmer's tongs, the journalist guessed), and their backs burnt with a cattle brand.

Then, in 1861, there was another small string of murders near the center of Pennsylvania. The women had been found with cut throats, and much like those in the previous article, had their eyes removed. All were found branded.

In 1871 there were more, but now having moved west through PA, near Harrisburg.

1874... 1879... 1884...

Wolfe spun the wheel faster and faster. Sweat dampened his armpits. His breathing was labored.

1901... 1909... 1916...

Ahead, again.

1939... 1948... 1952...

Stopped.

In 1952, in Cherry Brooke, near the border of Ohio and Pennsylvania, the police found three women on the lower south side. Their eyes were removed, throats cut, and were branded on the back of the neck, lower back, and chest respectively. Low quality photographs accompanied the article but were too small to make out anything clearly.

He moved on to 1958.

Again, the same read-out, as though copied from the previous ones.

1962... 1968... 1970...

Then, either the killings ceased, or the news stopped covering them. He went ahead to 1990. *Must've missed something.* He scrolled back, read through from 1971 to 1990 once more, finding nothing. Noting the time gap, he continued until 1994.

An obituary for Johnathon Acerieas Jr was published on January 28, 1994.

Wolfe licked his lips. He pressed into the viewfinder, as though he could be anymore closer to the text. His heart slammed in his chest.

Johnathon Acerieas Jr.

October 11, 1948 — January 28, 1994

Johnathon was a loving, caring husband to Donna Acerieas, who passed away in 1989, a dutiful father of Gregory, and grandfather of William. He served in the Vietnam War and generously donated funds to the Cherry Brooke Public Library, gave artifacts and books from his travels to the Cherry Brooke Museum, and served on the board of directors at Cherry Brooke University since its founding in 1967. His grandson, William Acerieas, survives him, and is left with his family home in the city.

Wolfe didn't realize he wasn't breathing. His face prickled with numbness. He let in a gasp of air, almost choking, and slowly brought his breathing under control. It was circumstantial, didn't prove anything, yet there was something here. He had to find William, had to question him, see if he had any information that would point him in the right direction, if there was another direction to go. He could be the end.

He wrote down the grandson's name, set the book aside, closed his notepad, and stood up. His legs buckled, having gone to sleep during his search, and he nearly tumbled into the filing cabinets. He half-walked, half-limped, back to the front desk. The librarian was reading a book, but looked up as Wolfe approached her.

"Find everything you need?"

"I did." He looked out the doors into the night. "Don't you close before six?"

"Typically, we do, but you were the only person in today." She sighed. "Ever since Mrs. Davis's passing, not many have been coming in."

He reached over the counter and patted her hand. "It'll pick up, don't worry. People will forget what happened and come back."

She smiled. "Hopefully."

"Thanks for everything, and I'm sorry for what happened. Have a good night."

"You, too."

Droves cheered on the sidewalks. Shouted out of apartment windows. Cars honked. Restaurants were open past closing, owners at their open door pulling in laughing customers. It was New Year's Eve in the spring, without the confetti and glitter.

What the hell's going on?

He stopped at a red light and looked to the TVs that filled a display window, all playing the same news station. Wolfe rolled down the window. Looking through the gaps of those standing in front of the store, he saw a newsroom, journalists filling every seat. Wolfe thought it looked like Conti, the commander, the mayor, and some other guys from the precinct taking the session, but wasn't sure.

A car honked as the light turned green. He called Wilkinson as he drove, hoping he'd be able to do him one last favor. He winced as chanting and hollering on the other end deafened him. Wilkinson shouted into the phone as Wolfe pulled it away from his face. "Did you hear? Did you hear?"

"What happened? It's one giant party out here."

"We got him! We finally got him!"

"Who... *shit*!" He slammed on the brakes. A group of young people jaywalked to the other side, laughing, jumping, smoking. A man on a bicycle zipped past before Wolfe pressed on the gas. "Who did you get?"

"SSK! Walter Francis Buks! That's his name. Walter Francis Buks. WFB. Middle-aged schmuck who worked at *Tuxedos and More* up on the lower west side, can you believe it?"

"That's great, Wilkinson, that's great," he said, grinning. He wanted all the details, but later. He didn't have time to be excited or learn all the details. He was too close to the end of his own crusade, and he could ask about SSK later. "I'm happy we finally got him, and I hate to ask now, of all times, but—"

"He's *only* in his thirties but looks like a skeleton. Flabby. Pale. Like that crypt keeper guy on *HBO*. It doesn't feel real, feels like a dream."

"Wilkinson."

"Oh, shoot, sorry, sure, I'd do about anything right now! Haven't felt this good since I got married."

"Can you get me the address of a Johnathan Acerieas Jr?" He drove around aimlessly, trying to get away from the crowds and the noise. Sidewalks started to empty, shopping complexes replaced by close-knit communities and quiet homes. Lights were on inside in many of them, people standing or sitting, glued to the TV. Everyone had every right to celebrate, but Wolfe couldn't help thinking about his own task. *It's only one murderer. They don't know the half of it.*

"Tell you the truth, even my wedding night doesn't feel as good as now. God bless my wife's soul. I feel like I can fly! Gary, the station's going out for celebratory drinks tonight. On me! Are you coming? Say that you're coming."

"Can't. Have something to do, sorry. That address, Wilkinson?"

"I'll get it to you in a second."

"Great, thanks. Just call me with it."

"Will do. God, Gary, we got him, we finally got him!"

Wolfe hung up and parked under a street lamp. Fifteen minutes Wilkinson called back. The station was still in a frenzy, but he made out the address over the ruckus. Wolfe thanked him and ended the call.

The address was ten miles away.

He dropped the phone into the cup holder and pulled out. Cherry Brooke finally had its killer and, for a while, they could feel safe again.

It was his turn to do his part.

William

He checked the tubing that ran from the discs under the vats to the machine, and then the cords to the generator in the back. Then, setting the generator on low, William allowed the vats to warm and simmer. The lever near the door, the one his grandfather used years ago, still worked. That morning, he had tied a rope around it and brought the end of it to the chair, so that he could pull it while bound. He wouldn't be able to tighten one of the three straps, but he decided it would be fine.

William sat on the stool in the side-room with the tranquilizer gun in his hands. Three darts were inside, filled with the unnamed concoction his grandfather made.

He didn't have the energy or the strength to find someone else.

It has to be me.

Wolfe

A Victorian house came into view in his headlights. He turned off the car and peered up through the windshield. The night enveloped the house and masked most of its details, but the streetlight caught the white trim, the crimson paint, the wrap-around porch and pointed turret.

He popped open the glove box and pulled out the 9mm pistol he kept there for safety. Cindy hadn't wanted it in the house when Tabby was born, so he put it here. He was relieved that Conti hadn't known about it after he confiscated Wolfe's station-issued Glock. He freed the magazine, finding it was fully loaded, and slapped it back in. Pulling the chamber, he checked for a round, then pocketed the gun. Wolfe got out of the car.

His body tingled with anticipation, his extremities waking from a deep sleep. Around the car, up the stone walkway, the small set of stairs, and to the front door. There were noises inside. They sounded mechanical, accompanied by a bubbling, like water left on the burner.

Wolfe tried the legal way first, so he knocked. He'd speak to William, get an idea of who he was and how he acted, and go from there. He could be wrong, after all. The evidence wasn't entirely fool-proof, and if it was brought to court, it would be deemed circumstantial. If worst came to worst, at least he could say he *tried*, though little good it would do.

A few minutes later he knocked again. He shuffled from one foot to another. A couple more moments passed and he gave up. He crept down the stairs and around to the back of the house. Wooden stairs lead to the back door. He knocked harder this time and waited. When no one came, he tried the doorknob. Locked.

Damn.

He peeked through the window but couldn't see any lights on.

Wolfe tried the door again. It didn't give. Applying more pressure, it gave a little. Wolfe glanced over his shoulder. The yard was empty and quiet, and there was no neighboring houses close enough to hear. Still holding the handle, he rammed his shoulder into the door. The wood snapped like bone. Wolfe slipped inside, crouched, and closed the door.

"Hello?" he called. "Anyone home? Cherry Brooke Police Department." He thought up a lie. "We got a call about a disturbance."

No reply.

He crab-walked to the adjacent wall and drew the pistol.

"Hello?" he repeated.

There was an outdated stove but it was cold. *Where's that boiling coming from?* A kitchen table in the center, two chairs, cabinets above and below, a fridge in the corner. His fingers tensed, waiting, waiting.

No one came running. No sound of movement anywhere in the house.

This place abandoned?

At the doorway, he peeked around the corner. A door was midway down the hall and at the end, another room opposite the stairwell. He checked the door and found a laundry room, clothes heaped on the floor. Past the banister, he took aim. No lights. No sound. The living room was empty save for a threadbare couch, two faded wooden chairs, a grandfather clock, and inlaid shelving around a dark stone fireplace. Wolfe imagined dust and cobwebs covering everything.

The bubbling noise was coming from beneath him. Something was boiling in the cellar.

Wolfe stretched his back and entered the room ahead of him. Sliding doors were set into the far wall and, cautiously, he slid one open.

Stopped.

Four wrought iron pedestals stood in the corners, tall lit candles burning on top, casting a dim glow over the floor-to-ceiling bookcases stuffed with old books. A large podium was near the right wall. Carved, slithering lines ascended from its base, reaching over the brim of its flat top. A large, yellowed open book rested atop.

He closed the book to read its cover. It was bound in wrinkled, washed-out purple leather. Embedded into the coarse material with flowery lettering was the title.

"In abissum Incomprehensibilem et Ultra," he whispered. Below the title was the Acerieas's family crest.

He reopened the book.

It was written in a language he couldn't read, like the title. Wolfe didn't think it was a real language, like an amalgamation of several different languages, creating some bastardized tongue.

He flipped to a random page.

A full-page ink illustration of a nude woman lying on the family crest, her arms above her head, hands intertwined, and her bent legs crossed. Her eyes were gouged out and a line was drawn through her throat, black blood streaming down her body, filling the empty spaces of the crest.

Wolfe turned the page.

Pictures of abhorrent bodies, clearly not human. Gangly figures with wings made from arms, round, short things with eyes protruding from backs like tumors. Something four-legged with a mane of tentacles and long tail of fire, fading tendrils mimicking outer space with empty points for stars.

The detective flipped ahead again.

Italicized text he couldn't understand encircled drawings of geometrical shapes of varying size. Nothing else, just inklings of other places not of this world within the shapes.

Wolfe closed the book and tightened his grip on the pistol.

William

He wouldn't sacrifice himself lucidly.

The drug in the darts was powerful. He'd seen his grandfather's Offering fall unconscious in seconds.

Perhaps it numbed them before overtaking them. Perhaps it had some sort of painkiller or sedative?

He shook his head. It wasn't important what it had or what it did, only that it would intoxicate him enough to be the conduit. It's makeup, like nearly everything, it seemed, was unknown. The Family's foundation was built upon the creating the bridge and the teachings of the Book; the unquenchable thirst to create the connection and obtain the supposed power in the Other World, which they would use ascend from the humanity that shackled them.

You've been down this road before.

It doesn't matter now.

You're here and it's time.

Exhaustion blanketed him. He was too tired to even consider what unspoken skeletons may be in his Family's old, old closet. More than ever, he was prepared to fulfill his life's purpose.

Somewhere he heard a door open, but much like his thoughts, he ignored it.

Doesn't matter what it is.

I'll be gone soon.

Wolfe

He opened the small door, wincing as its hinges creaked, and found a steep, narrow stairwell. He descended slowly. The bubbling increased in volume the further he went until it was all he could hear. The stairs ended at a doorway cut from crumbling red bricks. Putting his back against the wall, he peered around the corner.

His jaw went slack.

The cellar was enormous. Thick wood pillars were embedded along the wall, jutting into and across the ceiling where large pouches of soil bulged. A pile of shattered glass lay at the bottom of the wall near an overturned ladder. In the center of the room sat two glass vats, brimming with a boiling, frothing emerald liquid. The vats sat on wide metal discs that illuminated the insides and, Wolfe guessed, heated the liquid.

Sleek tubes ran from their base along the floor, snaking towards a chair between the vats, and connected to a copper domed cap protruded from the headrest. Cracked leather straps were attached to the armrests and the front legs.

Wolfe wiped the sweat from his palms on his pants, one after another. He crossed the threshold and the frothing stopped momentarily.

Oh, God.

Eyes. Dozens, hundreds, of eyes rolling, bobbing, small, large, cataract, blind, thin strips of nerve stems trailing like fish tails from some, others perfectly round. Wolfe clamped his teeth together and forced the vomit rushing up his throat back down again. The grip of his gun dug into his palm. The world reeled briefly, and he closed his eyes.

One. Two. Three.

Opening them again.

To his right there was a small, lit room past another doorway. He waited for someone to come out but no one appeared. He forced himself to ignore the knotting of his gut and the vats of eyes, and moved ahead.

It was then that he saw the floor more clearly. Carved into the rock was a giant replica of the Acerieas's family crest.

William and Wolfe

Time passed. Minutes could've been hours and hours could've been days. William couldn't say. He hadn't moved from the stool, hadn't taken his eyes off the tranquilizer gun in his hands. He stood, knees popping. He held the gun loosely at his side and left the room.

William stopped.

A bulky, tall man wearing a wrinkled dress shirt and navy pants was pointing a real gun at him. He looked familiar, but he couldn't place him. William slid the tranquilizer gun behind himself, out of view.

The stranger swallowed. "Are you William Acereias?"

"And who are you?" He stepped closer and the man stepped back.

"I'll ask again. Are you William Acereias?"

William nodded and for some reason, laughed. More of a cackle than a laugh. He was lightheaded, the weight of his responsibility lifting from his weary shoulders. Only a moment ago he was ready to sacrifice himself, to give this life for his ancestors. Now, what he desperately needed had come to him.

This is a gift from beyond, too. They're still helping me. It may not be blood, but I don't care. "I was going to start the machine." *It's fate, destiny, providing one more offering.*

William took another step.

"Stop where you are."

William felt assistance coming from beyond, again, guiding the future, ensuring that he would succeed. *They won't let him shoot me.* His brow furrowed. A haze swirled in his head. Tired of talking. Tired of everything. It was time to begin. "Who do you think you are?"

WILLAIM WAS TALLER, YOUNGER, thinner, paler, than he was. Brown, greasy hair wafted across his jutting brow, stopping short of his eyes. He looked like he had been crying. His cheeks were more sunken than the composite the sketch artist had produced, but Wolfe spotted the chin and the thin lips. The way he looked like a fish. And more importantly, his arm was behind his back.

Wolfe didn't bother asking anymore questions or spurting out police bullshit. It was too late for that. It wouldn't change anything. He saw Cindy and Tabby in his mind. It didn't matter that the evidence wouldn't hold up in court. Wolfe knew in his soul that the man before him was the person who had murdered his family. "I was a husband and a father, and you took them away from me."

Musty cellar air warmed. Tension coated him like moisture. It was as though the world held its breath, waiting for the inevitable. William whipped a tranquilizer gun out from behind him and unloaded three darts into Wolfe's chest, like getting slugged all three times.

Wolfe fired back in reaction. Bullets ricocheted off the walls, chipped the floor, embedded into the ceiling. None of them hit the kid, ducking. The detective's head smacked against the ground, his gun skittering away. The world swam as blackness encroached his vision.

Fucking dart gun. They must be drugged. Bastard.

It was like being drunk underwater, like swimming in an ocean of chilled Vodka. He wanted to close his eyes and succumb to the numbness coursing through him, but he knew if he did, he might not be able to open them again.

Despite Wolfe's will, his eyes closed.

AFTER GATHERING HIS FINAL Offerings, tossing them in with the others, and strapping the man into the Machine, William cranked the generator's power to max and went to the lever. The vats furiously boiled and frothed. He had a flashback to his grandfather standing where he was. Was this how he felt when he used them? Did he feel that he was right, spending his son and niece like cartridges? Did the lever he held in his hand feel as bittersweet as it did to William? Using a life to save dozens, to evolve them into things unimaginable?

William prayed they were right. The stranger could very well be the conduit to give them a way out. He pulled.

The tubes spasmed like electrified snakes as the substance drained from the vats into the headset. The ground shook. A splinter shot through the Family Crest. Dust and dirt trickled from the ceiling and spilled down the walls. Floodlights winked out as a radiant light exploded through the room. William shielded his eyes with his other arm as he stumbled back.

AN OVERWHELMING SHARP, BURNING engulfed Wolfe's eyes. Searing agony surged through the detective's nerves, erupting in his brain and licking the inside of his skull. He thrashed in the chair, but something kept them in place. Then, as suddenly as the fire overwhelmed him it was extinguished, only to be replaced by a frigid numbness.

Bright, dull, vibrant and vivid colors, yellows and greens and blues and reds, bloomed from the absolute darkness. They swirled around him, intertwining into a storm of crashing chromatic waves. What held down his body disappeared. Everything that was solid around him vanished, as if the world burst into dust, casting him into an abyss. Colors dissipated like fog beneath the sun, revealing to him what was hidden all along.

THE LEVER RETURNED TO its resting position. Slowly, steadily, the light waned, the floor relaxed, the floodlights illuminated. William lowered his arm and took in the scene.

The man was slumped in the chair, his chin against his chest, limbs hanging like a ragdoll. Drool spilled from his open mouth; the cloth William had gagged him with by his feet. Nothing else. No portal. No bridge. No connection.

"Maybe it takes time?"

Seconds.

Minutes.

Nothing.

I've failed.

He stumbled towards the machine.

The exhaustion building up over the years had waited until this moment to crash upon him. His legs gave out mid-step and he fell. The cold of the cement felt good on his aching back. William closed his eyes, already at the brink of sleep.

I can't do this anymore.

Like dozens of blankets, a squeezing, comfortable cocoon enveloped him. His joints and muscles sighed with relief, and his mind eased for the first time he could remember. He had done everything in his power to fulfill his purpose. He hoped his parents would know that.

Please.

The overpowering emptiness of dreamless slumber came and didn't let go.

Gary Wolfe

WOLFE FLOATED UPWARDS ON an invisible current flowing from somewhere below, as though he were underwater debris being carried towards the ocean's surface. He pressed against a gelatinous layer of some kind, but the current forced him through. The substance bled into his mouth, nose, ears, and empty sockets until his lungs were full and yet he lived. His empty eyes brimmed with goo. Spheres and nerves and pathways weaved into the interior of his skull, connecting to what remained. His skull drained of the viscous fluid and when his eyelids peeled apart, he had eyes anew.

Something was lodged in his throat. Wolfe sat up and hacked up a ball of slick phlegm into his palm. He blinked and tried to make out anything in the darkness around him. His back was soaked, and he touched it only to pull his hand away, greasy and cold. He wiped the gunk on his pants and stood. Wolfe stumbled until he found his balance. Something like twigs crunched underfoot.

Where the hell am I?

A burst of soft lightning bloomed in the clouds overhead. The dense gray overcast illuminated Wolfe's immediate surroundings. Bones. Millions upon millions of bones of varying sizes and shapes smothered an endless desolate plain into the horizon. Heaps, piles, hillocks, remnants of life rising from the ground like cresting waves, broken only by crude, oily puddles.

Jesus.

Before Wolfe saw any more the light dissipated, plunging him back into gloom. A moment later the light appeared once more but farther away, his shadow stretching across the wasteland. Perspiration coated Wolfe's face and his heart raced. In every direction there was only death; no sign of life or places that might contain it. He was utterly alone in the vast necropolis, the light his the only marker.

Follow or stay?

Follow what?

To where?

He took in the field again.

Nothing here but bones.

The light vanished and, as darkness descended, a puddled bubbled. Faint, guttural words slithered from the water, gray spume lapping the rim. Feverish gibbering uncoiled inside his head, words skipping his ears entirely.

"Surgeix— bretida— Nuesabl'ee"

More water bubbled and the light vanished. He winced as the incoherent words pierced his eardrums like a high-pitched whine.

"Fergoi— Nuesabl'ee"

"Lidag— th'—"

"Nuesabl'ee— Nuesabl'ee— Nuesabl'eeeeeeeee—"

The language grated on his mind. Chilled hands slid down his back. Wolfe spun around, searching for the speaker of the rasping syllables. There was no one. The light came again, much farther away now, and Wolfe hurried after it. Light was better than dark, and far better than whatever filled his head with gibberish.

Bones popped and cracked underfoot. Some crumbled into dust. The dank air tasted rotten and burnt. He tried to avoid the puddles, but when the light disappeared a rib stung his calf, and he tripped, crashing into a jutting bone, ramming into his chest. Blood ran down his ankle, but he ignored it, getting up when he'd found his breath.

He thought of stopping but couldn't. The light had to lead somewhere, surely. It couldn't be there for nothing. Mercifully, the chanting grew fainter behind him. He could handle the dark, the emptiness, the endless pursuit, but not those piercing chants.

His foot slipped and he fell face-first into something huge. He reached out to break his fall, but his fingers smashed against stone and snapped back. Fiery, sharp pain lanced up his arm, but it was short lived when he cracked his forehead off a pointed edge. Crashing and tumbling, arms rag-dolling, down, down, down into unconsciousness.

Wolfe jerked awake. He was laying on the floor. His hand burned, likely broken, and his head pounded like someone banging on a drum.

He looked around him in the dim light. He was in a wide, circular room with a spiraling stairwell that narrowed as it wound up the walls, vanishing in the gloom. On both sides curved tunnels lead in opposite directions. Cross-shaped sconces filled with emerald fire lit the blue-gray stonework, and between the globes of light were cells behind black bars.

Taking a deep breath, Wolfe heaved himself up into a sitting position. Stabbing pain bolted down his back, and his gut burned. He touched the side of his head and brought his fingers away sticky with blood. He got onto his knees, then with one foot after another, stood. He used the wall for support through a wave of vertigo.

Each corridor looked the same, so he went down the one directly in front of him. Cells lined both walls from floor to ceiling. Now closer, he noticed the curved bars were jagged and rusted over. He didn't get too close to them. What light that did reach through the dense darkness of the cells shown dried purple splashed across the floor, scorch marks up one wall, and an inverted silhouette of something with long, thin limbs.

Wolfe inspected the adjacent cells as he walked. They were all empty save for the purple splotches on the floor and walls, and the inverse silhouettes on different parts of the space. Eventually he came to another stairwell, but instead of going up, they descended into a pit. Carefully he moved around the edge and peered into the void. There were no lights. No sound. A breeze wafted up and a foul smell burned his nose.

Clink.

Wolfe looked towards the corridor to his left and held his breath. His imagination, surely. His hands were jittery with anticipation. He waited in silence for a minute and, when the sound didn't repeat, he relaxed.

Clink.

Instinctively he went to shout, "Hello!", but bit his tongue. He ventured toward the arch leading into the pathway. He kept his back against the wall, reached for his holster to find it empty. *Damnit.*

Clink.

It sounded close. He peeked around the corner. Empty. Still on guard, he entered the corridor. The next clink was quieter, fainter. Wolfe paused before a cell, and the noise came again. He caught a glimpse of the thing inside and stepped back in horror.

A protruding brow cast shadows over the deep-seated ruby eyes of a creature lying on the floor. Purple blood seeped from slits beneath its eyes, some dribbling from its dark, open mouth at the bottom of its pointed face. Yellow-brown bruises covered its sickly fragile body and beaded gray flesh. Its claw was drenched in colorless fluid, and it held a jagged stone it hit weakly on the bottom of the grate.

Wolfe, nearing the cell, felt it wasn't a threat. It smacked the bars again. Strangely, he recalled being in a pet store with the girls, Tabby staring wide-eyed at the puppies behind the Plexiglas, knowing that if no one adopted them, they would eventually be put down. But this was far, far worse. The thing, whatever it was, was clearly a prisoner, abused to the brink of death. A five-year-old could snap it over their knee like a twig.

It stopped tapping, meeting Wolfe's gaze.

The detective knelt. "Can you understand me?"

"Uda'em." Its chest heaved; brow furrowed. "Uda'em soravure..."

It was pointless to ask about where he was, or how to get home. The policeman's kindness took over. "What happened to you?"

"Var'em... Var'em mied th'Nuesabl'ee..."

Wolfe leaned in.

A fine, ivory mist coalesced like filament in its eyes. It raised the trembling hand holding the rock and hit the grate.

Clink.

It pushed the rock through the space between the bars, clunkily rolled and stopping at Wolfe's shoe. He looked at the rock, then at the creature.

"Th'Nuesabl'ee—"

A noise issued from the end of the corridor. Wolfe pocketed the stone, and started to leave but halted, glancing back at the creature.

"I'm sorry," he said, then he moved quickly to the opposite end of the tunnel. He turned the corner and put his back to the wall. Wolfe had a thousand questions about where he was, but after seeing the beaten creature, he decided to play it safe. Who the hell knew what was coming?

Something clacked against the floor.

"Ugly, aren't they?" A man's voice.

Wolfe fought the urge to peek around the corner.

"Glad we aren't them." Another man's voice, deeper.

"True, but we're at least half."

"Rather be half than whole," the second voice said. "C'mon, help me get it out of the cell. There's an Offering later."

There was the sound of steel grating stone, then Wolfe heard shuffling, like something being dragged over the ground, and faint moaning.

"You think it'll be satisfied with this one?" the second voice said.

"Is it ever?" the other said. They laughed.

Their laughter gradually quietened as they left the hall. Wolfe waited until it was silent before sliding down onto his haunches. There were too many questions in his head, waiting 'till now to hit him.

They spoke English.

An Offering for what?

Where the hell did that kid send me?

A chill wrapped around his shoulders. His heart fluttered as his breath hitched. He tried to breathe in the clammy air but it felt thick in his throat. Everything he'd seen and heard and felt suddenly barreled over him: the bones plains, the light in the clouds, the catacombs, the prisoner.

"Calm down Gary, calm down."

In and out. Steady. Breathe.

He clenched and unclenched his hands, forcing blood to flow. Heat replaced cold, and his heartbeat settled. "Good, good. In. Out."

He stood. Checking around the corner and finding the hallway empty, he started down it. It was silence except his footsteps on the stairwell. He kept himself against the wall. The rot stench built up the deeper he went. He breathed through his mouth, but he still tasted the rancidness of the humid air. Eventually he put his shirt collar over his mouth, but it didn't help. The stairwell led to more halls and empty cells, save for the now-familiar purple splotches and inverse silhouettes burnt.

He didn't realize he was at the bottom and almost tripped, catching himself on the wall just in time. Wolfe stepped through a peaked doorway carved from the dark stone. Giant blue-gray pillars rose from the floor to a domed ceiling. He strained his vision to make out the design carved into it, a web of thin indents moving from one column to the other, forming wavering symbols encircling the top of each, rimmed with green light. The artwork on the glossy floor matched the ceiling. In the center of the room was a raised circular platform, on which sat a stone chair with rusted wrist and ankle shackles.

Wolfe slunk into the room and hid behind the nearest pillar.

"C'mon, move!" a man shouted somewhere off to the right.

The lights dimmed, submerging the bottom of the space in gloom.

A sterile white light exploded from above, basking the platform and people who knelt before it. Long shadows spread over the floor and obscured the faces filling the room. Wolfe could see that they were thin, however, and what clothes they wore were tattered and torn.

The creature from the cell was now bound to the chair on the platform, and Wolfe felt a stab of guilt in his chest. Its head lolled to the side, and it was bleeding from a gash in its head. Purple trickled from its nose and mouth. Its chest rose and fell weakly. It wore no clothes and, to Wolfe, seemed sexless.

"We present this Offering," a familiar voice said from the shadows.

The thing striding in the light wasn't a man. It had two thin legs and narrow arms, a round, hairless head, and a wide torso. Its flesh was the same blue-gray as the creature in the chair. Hollowed, purple eyes were above two slits that served as a nose, and it had two tiny holes on the side of its head, vibrating as it spoke. It had no apparent mouth. Held in its hooked fingers was a four-pronged, rust-streaked spear.

"To the Unseeable, the Almighty, the Light Behind the Clouds, we present this Offering to you for the security of the catacombs that those before us had built."

The man-thing left the platform. Stone ground against stone and the platform rose on a winding beam connected to the underside of the disc. The creature seemed to have already accepted its fate. Wolfe craned his neck to watch as the ceiling opened, revealing a pitch-filled portal, resealing once the platform passed through.

Wolfe pressed his back to the pillar. A thought wriggled its way from the recesses of his mind.

There was only one guard.

Weren't there two speaking before?

A high-pitched shriek. People gasped and moaned.

Then, something smashed against Wolfe's face, throwing him into the ground. His head bounced off the stone, and he tried to see what hit him, but he was struck again and everything went black.

Stone...

Emerald lights...

Black bars...

"New one, eh?"

Metal clanging...

Wolfe groaned, rolling over. Blood matting his hair.

Movement nearby. He tried to stand but his body refused to obey, muscles and joints disobedient. The ripe stench of musk, sweat, feces, and urine filled the warm air. He coughed into the floor.

"Another," a woman said.

"Wonder how he got here," a man said.

"Probably another failure, like all Acerieas."

"Did you say Acerieas?" Wolfe said, speech slurred.

"I did."

Wolfe opened his eyes. Smudges of shadows loomed over him. Blinking away the blurriness, the room came into focus. Soft green light came in through steel bars, and dirty, frail pale people in threadbare clothing sat on the floor. Something like a pebble moved in the back of his mouth. He spat out a bloody tooth, tumbling across the ground. "How do you know them?"

An old man laughed and others joined in. He limped from the wall to Wolfe and stood over him. A yellowed shirt hung loosely over shredded, striped underwear. His brittle body shivered. "Isn't it obvious? We're all Acerieases."

"Did you people make this place, then?" Wolfe rested against the wall, some strength returning to his limbs. His head throbbed. He considered bringing up Will and the murders, but in a room full of his family, he'd put himself in more danger than he already was. Better to play it safe.

The man shook his head. "It was here before we arrived, same with the Unseeable. Some think it was the Tokens that built them. All dead now. You saw the last of them in the cathedral, yes?"

He nodded.

"Shame, but maybe justified. They did imprison us first, after all... The real problem, however, is that damn book. Like giving a child a firearm and expecting nothing bad to happen."

Wolfe had too many questions in his head to answer, so chose a simple one. "How?"

The old man prodded his calloused palm. "That book gives instructions on how to create a bridge, tempting fools with a higher state of being and some sort of unimaginable strength. I'm sure the physicality of it all has changed since my time, but it would still work the same: harvest Offerings and use them to power the device. Some were stolen from laboratories and morgues, some torn straight out of fresh bodies." He sighed, scratched his forehead. "All failures, all of us. Before I was used, the family slowed their work. Too much attention, too many bodies washing up eyeless, you understand." He waved a hand in front of his face. "We've been here ever since."

"How long has it been?" *These were people in the articles. These are the ones who killed so many before even Will was born.* He flexed the hand, feeling returning to his fingers. *Not broken, at least. Wish I had my gun. Just to have to keep playing along.*

The man scratched his chin. "Decades, maybe? Time doesn't work quite right here. Our minds age but our bodies don't. It was 19-something when I was sent here. Doesn't matter, anyway. Our stories are the same. There's no power, no transformation of our earthly bodies. There's nothing but the Unseeable and the bone-ridden plain above us. Initially the Tokens controlled these catacombs—some sort of prison, I guess—and locked us up as we came across. Then there were more and more coming and then there was a revolt. We stole their weapons and locked them up instead."

His legs shook, so he sat. Wolfe instinctively drew his legs in to avoid touching him.

"But some thought the Tokens should be given a worse treatment, were Acerieas after all, didn't they know that? We were destined for godhood and how dare they do such a thing." He chuckled. "We didn't even know the Tokens had a sex, let alone breeding capabilities, but we soon found out. Half-breeds came days, weeks later. Ugly, hairless blue infants that turned into those guards out there. Thankfully most didn't survive birth. The ones that did grew fast and were hell-bent on ruling. A battle broke out, both sides with hefty casualties, but they managed to imprison the naysayers and the pacifists. And, that my friend, brings us here."

Wolfe looked past the old man to the others huddled in the opposite side of the cell.

No kids here.

No one under the age of twenty.

Guess they don't put children to the chair, but have no problem killing one to use it.

"More failures arrived and they were either arrested or just died up there. Now the last remaining half-breeds keep the to catacombs and use the Tokens as sacrifices for the Unseeable."

"You keep saying that. What is it?"

"The light in the sky. Surely you saw it when you came?"

Wolfe nodded.

"Anyone who's used doesn't come back."

"What happens," Wolfe asked, "when they run out of these Tokens?"

The man laughed. "We'll soon find out. The one you saw was the last of them."

Wolfe clenched and unclenched his hands as he digesting the information. The more he mulled over it; the more fear grew. Yet despite being in an entirely unknown world with new species, a vast graveyard above his head, and a cell full of history's murderers, Wolfe couldn't fight the urge to still want to help them.

It was the Acerieas's fault, but it also wasn't. Most would have been too brainwashed to see reality before it was too late. How many had the obscene doctrines drilled into them as children? How many were purposely kept from society all their lives, following the parents who were meant to protect them?

They didn't have to kill.

They could've said no.

It wasn't hard to imagine a kid refusing to leave all they'd ever known. Friends. Families. Life. What kid would give that up? What kid would question what they were taught right from the beginning? What kid would choose their own exile? However, he couldn't let go of William, of getting revenge for what he did. Those people might've done the same, but it'd seemingly been decades since then. He couldn't do anything about their victims now, here, but there was still a chance to do something about William's.

Worry about yourself, Gary. You need to get out.

He slipped his hand into his pocket and felt something solid. He removed the creature's rock, glinting as he rolled it in his hand. Suddenly, the room dimmed, and his chest felt light, tight. Sweat shone on his face. When he tried to lift his head, the cell slurred, and a wall of blackness hit him.

A gift in polka dot wrapping paper sat on the living room table. Cindy sat cross-legged with Tabby standing on her lap, her chubby hands on the table, leaning forward, looking at the gift with childish wonder.

Wolfe blinked and a cake replaced the present. Yellow and pink streamers twirled off the sides of the table, flowing over the floor. He smiled when Tabby giggled. She wore a party hat which slouched and almost covered her eyes.

A tear trickled down his face.

Wolfe reached to adjust Tabby's hat, but when his fingers met the cardboard it coated his hand, like grabbing a warm stick of butter, molding into another layer of skin. He wrenched his hand back in horror and found his hand soaked in red.

The room, the cake, the gift, Cindy and Tabby, all melted like wax. Their faces tore away, leaving empty voids. Their arms dripped from their shoulders, congealing with the bubbling ground below. He tried to scream but a palm clamped over his mouth, and he looked up to find William Acerieas looming over him, grinning.

The room shook and darkness descended. Tendrils rose from the nothingness in his family's faces, climbing over the table towards him. Wolfe struggled to escape, but the freezing tendrils slid up his arms and William began to laugh and everything became nothing.

"Are you okay?"

Wolfe lay on his back, cold sweat blanketing him.

"You fell unconscious and started crying," the old man said.

"I'm fine," Wolfe croaked. He wiped his eyes and sat up. "I'm fine," he repeated. "Is there a way back?"

Everyone in the cell laughed. "You think we would still be here if there was?" a woman in the crowd said.

"Some believe that becoming a sacrifice to the Unseeable would work, that its power could mimic the device and send a person back. A few tried but were killed before they reached the platform. They have only used Tokens, like I said. I think it's likely that if you're used as a sacrifice, you'll just be killed and that's it."

Silence fell over them. Then Wolfe said, "When's the next one?"

"A few days?" The old man shrugged. "Can't be certain here. And without Tokens, things may change."

No other way. It's die here or die trying.

But how do I try?

He imagined the cathedral, how the pedestal looked. There had to be a trigger or button or something that raised the pedestal, a device he didn't see before he was captured. If he was on the pedestal, someone would have to activate it regardless. Toddle would do it if he were here.

"Would anyone raise the platform for me?"

Wolfe had hoped the old man would offer, but he limped away into the shadows.

"Only an idiot…"

"Is he serious?"

"Just like the other imbeciles."

"A waste."

"He'll get us all killed."

"I just need, someone to turn it on," he said a little louder.

"No one comes back."

"I don't want to die."

"The Unseeable."

"I'll do it." A woman stepped out from an unlit corner. The others fell silent. Her pale, greasy skin was smeared with grime, and her short auburn hair was a tangled, matted nest. Her jeans were torn at the thighs, and her t-shirt only reached her protruding rib cage, under which was a sunken stomach.

"You sure?" he said.

"Just tell me what needs to be done."

"Idiot woman."

"Stupid girl, going to get us all killed."

The woman turned and, surprising Wolfe, shouted, "Will you shut up? You complain but refuse to do anything to help yourselves. We'll all die here eventually, so what else is there? If it works for him, tit could work for us." She faced Wolfe again. "What's your plan?"

Other than her, who introduced herself as Alicia, no one spoke to him. He moved to the farthest corner from the gate and waited. Wolfe sat apart from the group, and every time Alicia came to him and went back, less of them acknowledged her. By the end of what felt like a week Earth-time, nobody spoke to her anymore, so she stayed with Wolfe in his corner.

When she initially asked about his plan, he hadn't the faintest idea what he was going to do. Time passed and he was still clueless. He tried think like a detective back, but nothing came to him. Meanwhile the humiliating, degrading conditions in the cell continued, the small amount of slimy, doughy food given to them was difficult to swallow. Cups of oily water were given at random. Everyone relieved themselves in front of everyone else against one wall, and not everyone turned away.

His mind slowed and his thoughts sluggish. He barely recalled his past life, what his house was like, what car he drove, what anyone looked like except for Cindy and Tabby, and William Acereias.

"I know others have died trying, but what if we just ran for it?" Alicia said, propped against the wall. She pushed hair from her brown eyes. "If they didn't take those cups back, we could make them into a weapon."

The Token from the cell popped in his mind. He took the rock from his pocket, warm from his body heat, and held it up to her as though it was discovered treasure. "You think this could work?"

"Maybe. Maybe not. But it's a weapon all the same. In which case, the plan is basic enough. When we're taken into the hall when the half-breeds need to select someone to use, before they're put into the chair, we make a break for it." Alicia scratched the ground with a chipped fingernail. "It's not a good plan, though. They have spears and we have a rock. There's only two of them, but they're quicker and stronger than us."

Wolfe wished he had his gun, again.

"You could run interference." He drew a rough outline of the room in the grime on the floor and pointed to the pedestal. He made a line to a dot. "You get behind this pillar and stay behind there for cover, once I'm on the platform, you make a break for whatever makes it go up. That'll leave only one guard for me to deal with."

"What are you going to do against it?"

"I don't know. Try to hit it, or avoid it altogether. All I have to do is make it to the chair and you to the trigger. We might not even have to fight them, just cause enough confusion that they don't know what to do." He looked at the huddled group across the cell. "If only they'd help."

"They won't," she said. "That lot will sit and rot first."

"Look," Wolfe said flatly. "You could die doing this. I could, too. You sure you want to help? I wouldn't be mad if you didn't."

She glanced at the crudely drawn map. "We die out there or in here. It all comes to the same end, doesn't it? This way, at least there's hope."

Silence fell. Then she said, "How did you get here?"

Cindy.

Tabby.

Eyeless, blood, throat open, a gaping maw.

Branded.

William.

Wolfe cleared his throat. They knew he had been put to the chair, but to bring up it was one their own, one of their *children*, was too risky. He didn't want them to view him as an enemy. They had enough of that with the guards. "Wrong place at the wrong time. You?"

"After my husband was used, I was put to the machine by his father. I had a son. I remember his face, but I can't recall the name. Dainty chin, hair like his father's, eyes like mine used to be. I wonder how he's doing now." Her words trailed away. She sniffled. "When I came over, it was like how you found it. Bones, black puddles speaking gibberish, the light in the clouds. It took days to find one of the wells. When I came down here there were a few more half-breeds than there are now. They threw me in here."

"I'm sorry."

"Don't be," she said, "I found my husband. He was in here with the others. But somehow, they knew we were married and they took him away. Years ago. I haven't seen him since." She sighed. "We were all gullible, believing all that crap from his father about this world and how wonderful it would be. That stupid fucking book. We were idiots. Me more than the others. What mother abandons her son for a pipedream? What sort of mother does that make me?" She clenched her hands at her side. "Now I'm a prisoner to things whose ancestors couldn't keep their hands on their own species. Guess I deserve it."

"When did they come over?" Wolfe pointed to the others.

"I don't know. Time's different here. Broken. I'd guess maybe the '40s, maybe the '20s. The family has been trying to make the bridge since at least the 1800s."

"Oh," he said, acting as though he didn't already know that.

These people would be eighty in the real world, maybe even ninety, but they don't look anywhere near thirty.

His gaze drifted to his hands, his shirt... and an idea emerged. Quickly he peeled off his shirt and tore it in two, horizontally. His splotchy, pale skin of his dwindling gut shivered.

"What're you doing?" Alicia said in confusion.

Wolfe didn't answer. He slid the top part of the shirt back on, and tied one end of the bottom half into a knot. He dropped the rock into the fashioned pouch. Wrapping the open end around his wrist, he gripped the tail and spun it in front of him.

"This should work better," he said. "It's not much, but it's more than just a rock."

Alicia held out her hand and Wolfe gave her the sling. She spun it a few times and handed it back. "If only we had two."

He was woken by the sound of metal banging, and wondered if it was feeding time again, but soon realized he was wrong. One of the guards entered, prodding limp bodies on the floor with the end of his trident. Wolfe hid the sling in his pants before it got close and tied the top end to one of his frayed belt loops. He struggled to his feet and stood against the wall by Alicia, who was already up and staring at the ground. The guard ignored them.

"Get up! If you're not all standing, we'll send you all to the Unseeable. Would you prefer that?"

They queued up before the opened entrance and they were escorted from the cell, down the corridor toward a winding stairwell. One by one they descended, a guard at the front and rear of the line. The sling jingled against Wolfe's thigh with each step. When he reached the bottom, he slowed to allow Alicia to catch up. His stomach churned and his fingers trembled. It felt like his lungs were too small, and lightheadedness threatened on the horizon.

Wolfe glanced over his shoulder at Alicia, whose eyes were narrowed and her hands balled into fists. Before the guards noticed their silent communication, he turned back and continued the slow march. They proceeded through the arched doorway, and into the cathedral. They crossed the wide room with the giant stone columns, and past the thing that must raise it, a gray disc, protruding from the ground a few feet from the pedestal.

There it is. That's the button to work the pedestal.

The prisoners were pushed in front of the platform and forced to kneel. The guards whispered to each other, then one of them left. Wolfe slowly moved his hand into his pants, and untied the sling from his belt loop. He held its tail, keeping the heavier end between his legs. The remaining guard scanned them absentmindedly. Soon the second guard returned with a weighty chain, sliding against the stone floor. On the other end was a Token, stumbling and falling, the steel bound tightly around its neck.

The prisoners looked at one another. *There's more of them?*

"C'mon! Rise!" The half-breed jabbed with its trident. "Rise!"

It yanked the chain, wrenching the Token forward.

"Get up! The Unseeable waits!"

The Token tried to obey but its arms and back trembled, and it collapsed again.

The guard groaned. "You pathetic fools," it spat, throwing the chain down. It crouched, lifted the Token up with one arm, and turned back to the pedestal.

"Alicia," Wolfe whispered.

"Yes?"

"Now."

Alicia stood. The second guard aimed its spear at her. "What are you doing?"

She walked backwards with her hands raised. "Just taking a stroll."

The guard moved forward, the spear's prongs prickling with green electricity. "Get back with the others."

She shook her head. "I'm fine here, thanks."

Bolts of lightning erupted from the weapon, but she leapt behind a pillar in time. The green current danced over the stone, crackling like burnt kindling, leaving scorch marks on the pillar.

Wolfe stood and sprinted to the second guard. It dropped the creature and scrambled to unsheathe its spear from its back. Wolfe twirled the sling as fast as his aching arm could and smashed it over the half-breed's head. It dizzily stumbled, holding its face with both hands, and Wolfe cracked it over its head once more. The rock shattered inside the sleeve, and the half-breed sunk to the floor. Blood gushed from a crack in its skull.

The other guard spun and shot at Wolfe, who dropped to the floor, the electricity searing over him. He crawled frantically towards the platform. Scorching pain exploded though his back, his limbs spasming violently. He smelled burnt fabric and flesh. He bit back a scream, staggered to his feet, stumbled onward, pumping his weak legs. He got onto the platform and lunged for the chair.

"Alicia!"

She sprinted for the button. The half-breed raised its weapon and fired. She tried to dodge but the emerald electricity washed over her arm like water, getting the full brunt of the blast. She screamed. Green fog billowed from her body and when it vanished, only a limp, shriveled arm remained, dangling uselessly at her side. She kept going, weaving around another column, dodged more lightning, and leapt onto the trigger.

The lift started to rise and Wolfe, using the chair for protection, watched as the second half-breed slowly get back to its feet, blood running down its face, and joined the other. Between them they blocked any escape for Alicia. She backed against a column, bleary eyes desperately searching for space to get through. The guard removed its trident from its back, and both leveled them at her.

Above him, a section of the ceiling opened, revealing a wide void beyond. Alicia looked from the half-breeds to Wolfe and smiled. The crackling electricity brought her attention back to her demise. The power intensified, filling the surrounding air with runoff static.

Wolfe ran around the chair, shouting for the others to help, for the guards to stop, for someone, anyone, to do something to save her, but his words were lost. No one moved to help, no one shouted or screamed, not a soul looked away, but the Token, forgotten in the commotion, limped towards them, holding up its chain.

The platform entered the opening and the void consumed him.

He slumped into the chair and put his head in his hands.

She knew the risks.

But I should've done something. Anything.

The Token could've saved her, though. Might've gotten to her in time.

Impossible. They starved and beat it. It probably was killed after Alicia.

This could've been avoided.

Another person I failed.

Downward pressure pushed upon him, gathering strength as the pedestal rose. Stale, warm air replaced the dampness of the catacombs. Wolfe straightened his aching legs, letting his exhausted arms droop over the armrests. He felt like he had run a hundred miles and climbed another hundred. His muscles were taxed, his tendons threadbare, whole body too drained to do anything except allow whatever was going to happen, happen.

He faced the void.

Soon, another circular opening appeared, and the platform's speed increased. Wolfe couldn't move from the chair even if he wanted to. Through the portal, he was cast back into the upper, bone-ridden world. Thick clouds rolled over the sky, stretching to every horizon. White light flashed, vanished, flashed again, closer and closer. Feverish words echoed up from the ground, grating against his mind.

"Surgeix—"

"Bretida—"

"Neusabl'eeeeeee—"

Sharp pain erupted behind Wolfe's eyes. He hissed through gritted teeth, tasted blood. It left his eyes, burrowing into his skull. Hammers pounded on his temples; needles stabbed the nape of his neck. He tried to lift his hands to cradle his splitting head, but the speed of his ascent kept them pinned down.

"Fergoi—"

"Lidag—"

"Neusabl'ee—   Neusabl'eeeeee— NEUSABL'EEEEEEEEEEEEEEE—"

Wolfe tried to scream but only a gurgle escaped him. He closed his eyes and hoped that it would all be over soon, but it wasn't, and when he opened them, he was submerged in the clouds. Silence smothered the voices. He couldn't hear anything, not even his breathing, nor his racing heart. High above the clouds, the pedestal jerked to a stop, and he fell out of the chair and onto the platform.

He coughed and spat blood. A minute, two, passed while his body adjusted to the motionless platform, then he carefully stood again.

"God."

He was below, or above, the heavens of another existence, the world upside down and right-side up. A featureless, oily layer of sickly yellow and crimson blanketed everything overhead and underfoot. Rows of fleshy, knobby limbs dangled, stretching from one periphery to the other. The not-sky rippled like waves, bubbled like sand. A giant maw opened in the distance, and a waxy, muscular pendulum dropped out, an overfilled meat sack, flesh shifting to keep dozens of *things* in.

A burst of radiant white light consumed the world. Wolfe peered through the crook of his arm. Red veins scattered through the clouds, and the swinging limb tore through the layer above and halted just before the platform. Every swing of its hideous end threw fetid wind his way.

Hundreds of skeletal hands and teardrop faces pressed against the inside of the bulging end of the pendulum, leaving behind a flurry of raised indents, deflating and being replaced by more. A slit ran up its center and fatty tar vomited out. The surrounding skin churned as more and more prints were left and filled in, left and filled in. Then, the slit ruptured and thick, viscous fluid spilled out. Millions of claws grappling and peeled apart polished webbing, bone, and translucent membrane, desperate to escape. The sack bloomed, torn apart by an army of claws, until all was revealed to him.

Wolfe gaped at the titanic eye with its broken, hideous emerald iris, ebbing with misty light. Its empty pupil was absolutely black, a window into the farthest reaches of an abyss. The eye smoothly rotated in place, up, down, left, right, before settling on the man on the platform.

Wolfe's bladder and bowels emptied.

It saw *him*. It saw through and beyond him; beyond his mind and into his conscious; past his subconsciousness, the superego, ego, and the id, all fundamental tiers shattered. The very foundation of his being was dissected, mangled, chewed and regurgitated. Past, present, and future; memories and nostalgia; hope and joy. Everything Gary Wolfe was, had been, and might become, was rendered and abandoned in the mental tumult eviscerating his psyche.

Blood spilled from his tear ducts and mixed with the drool running down his chin. His brain was a burning pyre contained only by a splintering skull. Nerve endings screamed and marrow boiled as agonizing flames turned his skeleton into a conflagration.

Three foggy, spiraling seams drifted over the sclera, sickly yellow in the iris, turning white as they passed into the pupil. The segmented orb inflated, burst, and millions of gray-blue teardrop shaped heads exploded over Wolfe. Hooked fingers scrambled over him, tearing cloth from flesh, flesh from muscle, muscle from bone. They poured into his open mouth, nostrils, eyes, ears, any opening he had.

Every molecule of his being was a supernova, each atom imploding. Indescribable torture became his identity. But he could still somehow see, saw more than before. He was audience to the frenzied rape his humanity and discovered they weren't devouring him but *augmenting* him. They twined with his fibers, transforming him into something else, something new. The madness above the clouds, the Unseeable, became lined with chromatic aberrations, bathed in Technicolor, bursting with kaleidoscopic shimmering. A hellish rainbow with a pulse.

Wolfe smiled. Cried. Convulsed. His eyes failed him but still saw the inner workings of his mind. He became audience to the mass of creatures raising him from the pedestal to a jagged hole that had formed in the Unseeable's pupil. Up into a vortex of anti-color and of unseen dimensions. They tossed him in, and he fell up, down, somewhere.

Raw, animalistic ecstasy coursed through his veins. Immeasurable pleasure smothered his flesh and drained into newly birthed pores. Pressure built and built, expanding from the inside, filling out the physical husk of what remained of Wolfe. Even when he was whole again it continued, on and on until he climaxed with newborn emotions, sensations, sight and sound and taste and pain bursting free. Then, they ceased and in the void between one place and another, Wolfe drifted like space debris.

"Open your eyes," said the void.

He did.

Wolfe and William

Wolfe saw before his brain registered sight. When he opened his eyes, he could see everything. Worms dug in the dirt above, the earth beneath the cement floor. He saw the unspent bullets in his gun's magazine across the room. He saw the blood pumping through William's body as he sat with his back to him, hunched over a book.

William's thoughts whispered through his mind like his own, like he occupied the kid's brain.

What now?

There are only theories and illustrations of the after. Portals and doors and opening, bodies with a dozen arms or a hundred eyes or legs emerging from every crevice. Nothing tells me what to do now.

Grandfather would know. He'd take care of this.

He shook his head.

How would I know if the bridge was made?

He flipped the pages faster and faster.

"Nothing!" He slammed the book closed. He stood and turned to Wolfe, still limp in the chair. Used Offerings lay in a burnt pile in the vats.

Still hasn't moved.

Maybe I should be next now?

Attempt to make the connection myself?

Collect new Offerings? Could I do that again?

He coughed into his arm and wiped his lips with his sleeve.

You've been through this already.

It's over.

You failed.

A vibration ran through the room, though Wolfe saw it was not exactly the room, but the outlines of the parts that comprised the room, faint and colorful, unseen containers of reality, like the black lines of a coloring book.

The colors split further apart, reds and blues ascending, yellows and greens descending, leaving an emptiness in-between. Crimson tinged a looming sky, pressing upon this world, then the lines calmed and settled back together.

"Why doesn't anyone know anything about the After?" William stomped on the book. "It's all theories and drawings and useless shit!"

I didn't want to kill, but what else was I meant to do?

The only way to bring them back was to harvest.

Why couldn't have they fought grandfather? Why did they give in?

"It all comes back to the Overseers, to grandfather."

The older generations force the young to do their work.

I hate him. He should've died sooner.

He did this.

William took a shuddering breath.

They're gone. Everyone. It makes no difference who did what or who made who do whatever. I'm a failure and they can't be brought back. The boy stared at the ceiling. *It's not worth staying here. If that man could find me, the police can, too.*

The detective's limbs jerked. He belched.

William spun around.

"You're alive?"

He couldn't tell if the man's eyes were open, but, when William came near, jaw slackening, Wolfe knew they must be.

"Your eyes, they're different." William knelt before him.

Wolfe willed his unshackled hands to move, and they did. He grabbed the boy's arms.

Something thrummed in the back of his head, rippling through his brain. Weight built in his temples and spine. With each pulse his consciousness was drawn into recesses of his psyche he'd never known existed.

An image blotted out the cellar, the boy, everything. A cliffside overhanging a wavering void lapping at bleak shores. An insatiable yearning brought him to the edge. Not only did his mind desire it, but his body, too; a craving and curiosity he couldn't hold back. The nothing wasn't the absence of life, it was everything. It was life and death and existence itself. It wasn't there because of the lack of light, it was there because it dwelled there, chose to be there, shielding what lived underneath.

Wolfe gave in.

Plummeting through the gloom like a fallen angel, he emerged on the other side. He was confronted with rolling vistas of sleek black muscle and drooping appendages, a grotesquery of torn seams, of things undone, of masses disgorging blue-gray into the world. Hands and faces and oily, gibbering waters rose from bottomless chasms in the earth a family had prayed for.

WILLIAM COULDN'T REMEMBER WHAT the man looked like before, but it was not like this. His short, brown hair turned white. His eyes were deep, ashen pits with smoldering embers at the bottom. Gray tendrils blotched his face like paint exploding from the inside. They trickled down to his neck, reaching underneath his sweat-soaked clothes. His lips were scabbed and burnt, caked in dried blood. There were darker veins that moving under the tendrils.

William tried to wrench himself free, but his hold was like steel, fingers digging into his arm, crushing the bone.

This isn't right, this isn't what the connection was meant to be, it can't be.

The man's grip tightened and pain shot up his arms. The former slid forward; eyes locked onto the latter. William heard bones shift, grind, pop and snap, but the stranger's face didn't register the feeling.

Please. Someone. Anyone.

William dropped to his knees.

His chest bulged with fluid, and returned to form again. The man's body pumped with something William wasn't certain was blood. He spoke with an oozing tongue. "You don't know what I've seen, What I am." A coughing fit seized him, and tar bubbled from his lips. Bones snapped like twigs, and he released his hold on William. The sound of crunching reverberated off the walls, echoing up the stairs.

No one has that many bones.

He'd scream from that much pain.

This isn't a man.

Although he didn't want to admit it, a thought passed through his mind.

This is my fault.

I did this.

Burning spikes pierced Wolfe's skull.

The foul liquid gushed from his lips. Reality's outlines frayed, unmaking themselves to reveal a sinewy sky, bulbous ends carving through the air. The place within, the place beyond. It tilted, upturned, revealed to him that the veined clouds he once stood above were no longer there, replaced by spiraling pillars. An ichorous sea smothered the necropolis below. Briefly he registered what it meant for those still in the catacombs before frantic gibbering gushed from the frothing sea. White latticed across the crimson sky, and the horizon ignited with blinding light—

"Stop," he groaned, heavily shaking his head. "Please don't."

He closed his eyes but saw through the eyelids the intertwining lines once more. The sound of breaking bones dwindled into quiet. Something moved. Wolfe raised his face to find William creeping towards his gun. He was crying, a stupid boy playing an adult's game.

A young boy... Dainty chin, dark hair, eyes like his mother....

William kept his sight on Wolfe and retrieved the gun. It looked too big for him. The boy knew his way around weapons, knew he was good with knives, blowtorches, brands, but the 9mm was comical in his hand. He pulled the hammer back and aimed it at Wolfe.

"This wasn't how it was meant to be," he said, hand trembling. "It was meant to create a portal. My parents were to come back." He wiped his tears away. "But you've come back a monster."

More pitch oozed from Wolfe's mouth. "I could say the same damn thing about you," he managed to say when his throat cleared. "Killed all those people, killed Cindy and Tabby. For this." He tried to raise his arms but they were too heavy. "Isn't this what your stupid family worked for? You did this."

Wolfe clenched his bloated hands. Oily sweat seeped from his pores.

"No," he blubbered, "no, I didn't. I didn't! I was doing what I was told. I didn't want to kill your family but it's my only purpose, my family's lineage, what else was I meant to do?" He fell into silence, then: "It's my fault, I know that, but I can start again. No more Offerings, no more brands, no more machine, no more Family. I'll change my name. Move away. Do good in the community."

Wolfe's chest rumbled, his throat rising. He prepared to hold back whatever was coming, but he laughed. At first, he was surprised, but he laughed again. It felt good. He laughed until sludge clogged his esophagus. "You can't do over after something like this—" The rafters vanished, outlines returning.

Skeletal arms raked up from the lifeless sea. The overlapping lattice in the red sky ceased in the center of an empty circle. The Unseeable fell from the abhorrent heavens, splitting at every seam, unloading waves of sacrificial chum into the waters.

"You can't go back," he said. "Once you get the ball rolling; it keeps going until the end. Your mother learned that." Treacle trickled from his nose. "She helped me, but no one's going to help you." He spat out burnt phlegm. "You killed my family, and I'm going to return the favor."

The ceiling dissipated. The empty circle was now the reverse image of the interior of an eyeball. Wolfe felt as if he was inside someone's head, peering out. Red veins scattered through the pinkish red orb. Abominations climbed the gore, dug into the Unseeable's meat, fusing together until they were towers themselves, retching ruby-tinged teardrop faces.

"It won't even be me who does it," Wolfe said. He slumped onto the floor, face-first. Wolfe didn't want to see the only place he ever knew be devoured. All he wanted was Cindy and Tabby. To see them smile and laugh and talk, to feel his wife's body against his, to carry his daughter as he ran his fingers through her chestnut hair. He wanted to do anything and everything and nothing with them.

Bubbling incessantly, the veins carried the tar through him. Wolfe didn't fight it anymore. He was too exhausted to carry on. What was done was done, and whatever the fucking thing had impregnated him with screamed to consume, to release, to bridge the gap that the Aceriases had desperately searched for.

With a sigh, Gary Wolfe let it through.

WILLIAM WAITED HIM TO move, but after a few minutes, when air escaped his mouth, he stilled.

Did he say my mother helped him?

Is she there?

In the Other World?

Is my father?

Is there a chance to bring them back?

No more breaking bones. No more fluid poured from him.

The gun in William's hand rattled.

He shook his head.

It doesn't matter now.

I can't do anything for them here.

I have to get out of Cherry Brooke before anything else happens.

William held the gun to his side, and walked backwards towards the stairs, keeping his eyes on the body just in case. He placed his foot to the bottom stair, about to climb. A quake shook the ground. He gripped the banister as the shaking grew stronger. Upstairs, dishes and framed photos dropped and crashed. Stonework split and cracked. But, underneath it all, there was the sound of rampant tearing, like thousands of paper reams being shredded.

Slick tendrils ripped from Wolfe's back. They burrowed into the ceiling, wrapping around the rafters. Purple and black ooze flooded from his wounds, quickly filling the cellar. William aimed the 9mm at Wolfe. The substance reached the chair, reached the vats, submerged the helmet, tubing, and the generator.

Wolfe rose into the air, dangling like a marionette from the limbs. William tried to look away but couldn't. Hooked prongs unfurled from his gaunt frame, and his clothes fell in drenched tatters. A mangled seal ran down the center of his swollen body, tiny rivulets of the liquid escaped as more and more fatty protrusions inflated the body.

William's stomach dropped but he pulled the trigger through the terror until there was a metallic click. Vats imploded, glass and leftover Offerings slopping over the murky pool. None of the shots hit him. The chair his grandfather loved was soaked through before it crumbled into mush. William chucked the gun at the madness as he struggled to stand and run but couldn't, tried to move only to realize that his legs weren't numb, weren't asleep, but were covered up to his shins by the ichor.

He tried to free himself but the stuff touched his fingers with frostbite. Slowly it rose to his knees. "Please! Please someone help me!"

Wolfe groaned.

The boy stared into the firepits replacing the man's eyes. The world lulled. In the silent, timeless moment, sound and feeling were gone. In this limbo between one second to another, William peered in horror at what he'd been born for, trained for, used for. This was his entire existence. He was terrified. The long-awaited connection had been made. Time caught up with them.

What rotten meat still clung to the detective's bones was torn apart like fabric. William had a split second to see through the bridge in Wolfe's chest into the Other World, the place his Family worked towards. There was only oily flesh, mountainous pillars spinning in a black sea, a maelstrom of never-ending mayhem and never-ending misery. The reverse eye beyond looked to him and blinked.

This isn't what the Book says.

This isn't what grandfather said.

That isn't heaven.

Worse than hell.

They can't be alive there.

A brilliant radiance boomed from the god-eye and devoured William's sight. Tiny claws quickly climbed through the thick fluid and scurried up his body, digging into his mouth. His brain soon became mangled. Lifted by the Unseeable into the air, William's corpse was carried into the open limb waiting on the other end. Pulled through, he became what he always felt he had been to his grandfather.

Nothing.

THE GENERATOR EXPLODED.

The Unseeable shrank back through Wolfe to its home of hell and bones. His flesh healed without a scar. Tendrils released the rafters and retracted into his body. Wolfe dropped and sank to the black bottom, coming to rest by the infamous Book. Flames streaked into the side room, devouring everything in its path. Soon, the gas canisters would explode. It tore up cellar stairs, rampaged through the study, and devoured the ancient books, the pedestal, the living room, its old furniture. All burned. The ceiling gave way and the attic crashed into the fiery pool below.

Now there were more sons and daughters. There were no more grandsons and granddaughters. No more nieces and nephews, not a single willing soul to read the Book and continue the Family's gruesome work. It was over.

Wolfe had one final thought.

Good.

ACKNOWLEDGMENTS

Thanks to the Grendel Press team for taking a chance with this book, and with all their help shaping it into what it is today. Also, I'd like to thank all the editors I've worked with over the years, I would be a much, much, worse writer without you.

Thanks to JT, JD, and the Kids. Even though I hardly show it, I always appreciate your support.

Thanks to the alpha and beta readers for reading this story when it was such a mess: Michael D., Maurice R., and Perry L.

Thanks to all the supporters on Patreon, you guys keep the lights on: David S., Jocelyn C., Rosina S., Calluna A., Shaun R., Black Book Sculpts, Claudia C., Kylie L., Nik C.

Thanks to the weird lit/horror community for always being supportive to every writer, known or unknown. Special shout outs to the folks on Twitter, the Books of Horror group, r/Weirdlit, Tenebrous Press, Shortwave Press, WeirdPunk Books, and all the authors I've met from Pittsburgh.

Unfortunately, I can't list everyone, but the people I've befriended over the years deserve their own mention (no particular order): Gwendolyn Kiste, Scott J. Moses, Kyle Winkler, Matt Wildasin, Elford Alley, Emma Editrix, Robert

Ottone, Sara Tantlinger, Katherine Silva, Michael Wehunt, David Peak, Alex Woodroe, Matt Blairstone, Alan Lastufka, RJ Murray, Orrin Gray, Sam Richard, Joe Koch, Sarah Budd, Mindy Rose, Beth Djonne, Nick Roberts, Zach Graham, Cina Pelayo, Briana Morgan, Matt Vaughn, and so many others.

About the Author
Micah Castle

Micah Castle writes speculative fiction. His stories have appeared in various magazines, websites, and anthologies. He's the author of Reconstructing a Relationship, The World He Once Knew, A Home in the Darkness, and The Women Without Eyes.

While away from the keyboard, he enjoys spending time with his wife, playing with his animals, being in the woods, and can typically be found writing or reading a book somewhere in his Pennsylvania home.

You can find him at: www.micahcastle.com, www.patreon.com/micahastle, or on other platforms: www.linktr.ee/micahcastle.

CONTENT WARNING

Violence, violence against women, child harm

For any victims and survivors who need support, the National Domestic Violence Hotline is there for you, 24 hours a day, 7 days a week. Call 1-800-799-7233 or 1-800-799-7233 for TTY, or if you're unable to speak safely, you can log onto thehotline.org or text LOVEIS to 22522.